BartLett
aɴᴅ tʜᴇ
forest of
PLeɴty

BartLett
and the
forest of
PLenty

by **ODO HiRSCH**

iLLustrated by

aNdRew McLean

BLOOMSBURY
CHILDREN'S
BOOKS

Published by Bloomsbury, New York and London
Distributed to the trade by Holtzbrinck Publishers

Library of Congress Cataloging-in-Publication Data
available upon request
ISBN 1-58234-931-2

Printed in the U.S.A.
1 3 5 7 9 10 8 6 4 2

Bloomsbury USA Children's Books
175 Fifth Avenue
New York, NY 10010

All papers used by Bloomsbury Publishing are natural, recyclable products made
from wood grown in well-managed forests. The manufacturing processes
conform to the environmental regulations of the country of origin.

1

In the walls of the canyon, time had laid down the rock like layers of a cake. Bands of white, yellow, red and brown stone pressed one upon another. To stand on the floor of this chasm and tilt your head back and let your eyes climb the layers up to the top, up to the dizzying height where the rock ended and the piercing blue sky began, was to read a kind of history. It was a history that dated back not decades or centuries or thousands but millions of years, to a time when dinosaurs walked the earth. And the dinosaurs were still there. From within the stone, exposed by wind and rain, their skeletons protruded—a spine, the long curving fragments of a tail, the knotted knuckles of claws and feet—now turned to stone themselves. High in the walls, the empty sockets of their skulls gazed down at anyone who walked below.

But very few people had ever walked there. The chasm was the Gircassian Rift, the deepest, longest canyon in the world, running through the earth like the cut from a knife. Around it was a vast desert in which no one lived. So there was little point coming to the Gircassian Rift, except to see the canyon for itself, and this was something that hardly anyone had done, only explorers dedicated to discovering the most isolated and difficult places. And as for what lay *beyond* the Gircassian Rift . . . even fewer people had tried to find out.

At the bottom of the canyon, there was a peculiar stillness. It wasn't complete. A stream trickled with a faint murmur. And there were pools of hot water, steaming with the earth's heat, that fed the stream and sometimes erupted in squelching bubbles. Yet between each trickle and squelch, there was silence, and all the way up, past the towering walls of the canyon and then out over the immense, empty desert, there wasn't a sound. The sky was clear and cloudless, with a blue intensity. Eagles soared, hanging high in the air with outstretched wings, riding the currents of hot wind. From the floor of the canyon, beside the stream, the eagles appeared as tiny black specks, if they could be seen at all.

But an eagle's vision is much sharper than that of a human. And you can be certain that, on one particular day, every eagle hanging in the air above the Gircassian Rift had spotted three people, who were climbing up, past layer after layer of rock, from the bottom.

The three explorers moved slowly, zigzagging up the wall of the canyon. Bartlett led the way. He was thin and wiry, with lean, stringly muscles and a freckled face. The well-worn boots on his feet were as creased and creviced as a turtle's neck, and his fingers, gripping the rock, were strong and knobbly. Behind him came Gozo, who was barely more than a boy, with a little upturned nose and hair that stood up in spikes. And last in line came Jacques le Grand, a giant of a man whose powerful shoulders were broad enough to carry any burden.

There was no path for them to follow.
Bartlett picked his way from ledge to
rock to niche. Sometimes,
when he couldn't see
another foothold, he
would look down at
Jacques, and wait
until the big man
had examined
the wall as
well.

Then
Jacques would
point, or tilt his
head, or even just
indicate with a glance
where he thought they
should go. There was hardly
ever a need for words between
them.

If Gozo couldn't manage by himself,
Bartlett would reach back down for him, or
Jacques would push him up from behind.

They had been following the Rift for over a
week, and now they were reaching the end. Once they had
climbed out of the canyon they would be able to see what
lay beyond it. There were rumours and myths. Bartlett
and Jacques knew them all, of course, they had heard all
the stories and speculation. But even they didn't know
what they would really find when they got to the top.

Steadily they made their way up from the canyon floor. Sometimes, to the eagles hovering high above them, they must have looked like gigantic lizards, as they stretched upwards to raise themselves further, and sometimes, as they held on against the stone with arms and legs spread, they must have looked like gigantic crabs. They had started the climb at dawn, but because of the great depth of the chasm, and the difficulty of the ascent, it was near dusk when Bartlett finally put his hand over the lip of the canyon and pulled himself out.

A moment later Gozo and Jacques were standing beside him. The canyon gaped at their feet. But they weren't looking down. Northwards, at last, they could see what awaited them beyond the Gircassian Rift.

2

'Trees!' cried Gozo excitedly. 'Look at it. Trees! Nothing but trees!'

Bartlett nodded. They found themselves, at the top of the Rift, on a bare, windy plateau overlooking an enormous plain. All the way to the horizon the plain was carpeted in a dense expanse of trees, without gap or interruption, except for a river that snaked through the forest, curling into the distance and glimmering like a silver ribbon that had been carelessly tossed across a thick, dark mat.

'You said there'd be a forest,' continued Gozo, 'but look at this, Mr Bartlett. I've never seen so many trees! It's so . . . so . . .'

'Green?' said Bartlett.

'Yes. I would have thought of it if you'd given me a minute.'

Jacques le Grand raised an eyebrow. Gozo was always thinking of things he would have thought of if someone had given him another minute. Jacques sat on the ground and pulled the cork out of his water bottle. He drank just enough to quench his thirst, not wasting a drop.

Bartlett sat down and drank from his bottle as well.

'No. It's not really green, is it?'

Bartlett and Jacques looked up at Gozo, who was still standing, gazing at the plain.

'It's almost black. That's what it is. *Black!*'

'You should drink something, Gozo.'

Gozo sat beside them and took a sip from his water bottle. But his eyes were still on the plain. 'Just think,' he murmured, 'there's a city in there. An ancient city, just waiting to be rediscovered.'

Bartlett sighed. That was just one of the stories, one of the many myths and rumours about the forest beyond the Gircassian Rift, and from the moment Bartlett had told it to Gozo, one morning when they had been walking beside the stream at the bottom of the canyon, he wished he hadn't done it. He should have known that Gozo would believe it, as if every word were proven. But wherever you went in the world, you'd hear a similar story about any deep forest or jungle which few people had explored. It was always the same, there was always some ruined city lost amongst the trees, temples roofed with silver, storerooms filled with gold, statues of idols with jewels for eyes. If an explorer went looking for every ruined city in every jungle he heard about, he'd never have time to explore anything else!

'It's just a myth,' said Bartlett gently.

'Maybe it's true,' said Gozo, staring at the plain.

'No. It's not true.'

'How do you *know*, Mr Bartlett?'

Bartlett didn't reply. There were only three things that anyone *knew* about the forest that lay below them on the plain. The first thing was that somewhere on the other side of the forest, when it finally came to an end, was the sea, a long strip of empty coastline where no one lived. Exactly how long it would take to reach the sea was undetermined, but it would take many days, if not weeks, and if you succeeded, the only way out would be to turn around and cross the forest once more in the direction from which you'd come, because no ships ever called at that coast. The second thing was that no one ever *had* crossed it—or at least, none of the explorers who had tried had returned to tell the tale. And the third thing was that there *was* no third thing, or fourth thing, or any other thing that was known about the forest that stretched before them.

Jacques was gazing at the long, sweeping curves of the river that curled across the plain. After a moment he glanced at Bartlett. Bartlett nodded. Jacques was one of those people who rarely speak, but for every word that passed his lips he thought ten times as many thoughts as any other person. He and Bartlett had been friends for so long that when Jacques wanted to say something to him, a glance was usually enough. It was Bartlett who did the talking.

By now Gozo knew them well enough to realise that their most important conversations happened without words.

'What is it?' he said, looking at each of the explorers in turn.

'We'll follow the river, Gozo,' explained Bartlett. 'If we're going to cross the forest, that's the best way to do it. If we follow the river, we'll get to the sea, and then we can follow the river back again.'

'But if we follow the river we might miss the city!' exclaimed Gozo. 'What if it isn't beside the river? It's in the trees, you said so yourself.'

Bartlett didn't reply. Jacques glanced at him knowingly, as if to say *that's* what you get when you go telling stories to a boy as excitable as Gozo.

Suddenly Gozo jumped up. He put his hands on his hips. 'You don't believe it's there at all, do you? Neither of you. I know you don't!'

'Just where would you like to start looking?' muttered Jacques, waving his hand across the vast plain that lay beneath them.

Gozo frowned. He didn't know. Bartlett and Jacques were the experienced explorers. *They* should be able to tell.

'Gozo,' said Bartlett, 'you have to understand what it's like to be in a forest like that. You think it's easy, but it isn't. It's dark. It's cold. You have to chop out a path for yourself. You lose direction. You can walk in circles for days before you even realise you're doing it.'

'So you're scared? Is that it, Mr Bartlett? I never thought you'd be scared of anything!'

Bartlett smiled. 'We're not scared, Gozo. But we don't do things if there's no point to them. Do you know what Sutton Pufrock used to say? "There's a difference between being scared and being careful. If you're too scared you're a coward, if you're not careful enough you're a hothead. But if you can't tell the difference between the two, you're something that's even worse—a fool!"'

Gozo grimaced. According to Bartlett, there was a Sutton Pufrock saying for every situation. There were so many of these sayings that Gozo sometimes wondered how Sutton Pufrock ever had time to do anything but make them up. Yet Sutton Pufrock had been the greatest explorer of his generation, and had taught Bartlett everything he knew. He was old now, of course, and rarely got out of bed, but that didn't stop him telling everyone else what to do.

'You don't believe me, do you?' said Bartlett. 'Jacques and I have crossed the Moray Jungle, Gozo. It took us a month to cross it, and even then, I'd say, we were lucky to survive.'

'And it wasn't only us,' muttered Jacques.

Bartlett glanced at him silently.

'Was someone else with you?' said Gozo.

Bartlett nodded.

'Who?'

'It was a long time ago, Gozo.'

'Why don't you want to tell me? Who was it, Mr

Bartlett? Not Sutton Pufrock!'

Bartlett smiled. It wasn't *that* long ago. 'Elwood Tucker,' he said quietly.

Gozo frowned. Who was Elwood Tucker?

'Elwood Tucker might have been the greatest explorer of us all,' said Bartlett. 'Sutton Pufrock used to say he would, and for years I tried to prove him wrong.'

'*Might* have been?' whispered Gozo.

'He disappeared.'

Gozo stared at Bartlett. His skin prickled with apprehension.

'He could have been a great explorer,' Bartlett explained. 'He really could. But he was over-confident, Gozo, arrogant.'

'Vain as well,' murmured Jacques.

Bartlett nodded. 'He was, it's true. He had a magnificent head of hair, Gozo, jet black, and thick as the fur on a grizzly bear. If I saw him again I'd recognise him in an instant, even now, just from the hair on his head. He was proud of it. Proud of everything about himself, everything he did. Too proud. He could have been a great explorer, don't let anyone tell you he couldn't. Perhaps he *would* have been the greatest. But he began to think he was invincible. He became foolhardy, Gozo, he refused to recognise danger. It was as if he always had to prove that he was better than everybody else, as if each exploit had to be more difficult than the one before. Nothing we said could stop him. Eventually he wouldn't even listen to Sutton Pufrock. He began to go off by himself, no one else was good enough to go with him.' Bartlett paused. 'When an explorer starts to do that, there's only one way it can end.'

'And where did it . . . *end?*' said Gozo, his voice hardly even loud enough to be called a whisper.

Bartlett glanced at Jacques, who nodded, as if telling him to go on. Bartlett turned back to Gozo.

'Here.'

Gozo's eyes went wide.

'He came here, Gozo, to the Gircassian Rift. He told everyone he was going to go beyond it. But he never came back.'

Gozo was standing, gazing at the forest. Now the sky was darkening, the plain was plunging into shadow, and the distant curves of the river reflected the last rays of the setting sun. But Gozo couldn't stop thinking about the story Bartlett had told him, about the proud, arrogant explorer called Elwood Tucker who had gone beyond the Rift.

'Do you think he's still in there, Mr Bartlett?' he whispered.

'This was ten years ago, Gozo. He can't still be alive. If he had survived, he would have found his way out. No, Elwood would have done something foolhardy, dangerous. Left the river, perhaps, and set off in another direction, just to prove that he could do it. Right, Jacques?'

Jacques nodded.

'You can't do that by yourself. You *may* survive, but

you'll be lucky. Too many things can go wrong. Do you know what Sutton Pufrock used to say about that, Gozo?'

Gozo didn't reply.

'He used to say: "When you find yourself thinking you can do everything by yourself, *that's* when—"' Bartlett stopped. 'Gozo?' he said.

'Look,' murmured Gozo. He pointed across the plain.

'What is it?' said Bartlett. 'What do you see?'

'I don't know.'

Bartlett and Jacques stood up. They peered into the distance.

'What is it?' said Bartlett again. 'I can't see anything. Can you see anything, Jacques?'

Gozo dropped his hand. 'It's gone.'

For a moment longer he continued to stare out over the darkening plain. He had seen something, but what? Just for an instant, far off amongst the trees, Gozo had glimpsed something pale, white, like a piece of bone embedded in the darkness of the forest.

But if it was a bone, to see it from that distance, it must be gigantic.

'No, it's gone,' he said. 'I can't see it any more.'

'Maybe it was the river,' said Bartlett.

Gozo shook his head. It was a long way from the river.

'Maybe it was a branch of the river.'

'No,' said Gozo, 'it didn't look like water.'

Jacques glanced at Bartlett. *Didn't look like water?* And how did Gozo, the great explorer, know what water looked like from such a distance, in the middle of a forest, under the light of the setting sun?

The sun dropped. Soon it was dark. That night, they slept on the plateau, and before they slept, Gozo tried to describe—five times, ten times—what he had seen. Yet the best he could do was to say what he had said five or ten times already, that it was a flash of something pale, white, like the glint of a gigantic piece of bone embedded in the forest.

3

'It was there. Right there! It was, Jacques.'

Jacques le Grand looked at Gozo doubtfully. Now, in the morning, the plain was bathed in clear, strong sunlight. If there was anything at all to see out there, it should have been visible—unless, of course, there was actually nothing there in the first place, and Gozo had made it all up.

'I didn't make it up. I didn't! Mr Bartlett, you believe me, don't you?'

Bartlett didn't reply. He was gazing at the plain, trying to find whatever it was that Gozo said he had seen.

'I *didn't* make it up,' muttered Gozo, and he waited to see what Bartlett would do.

Eventually Bartlett stopped looking. 'I can't see it,' he said. 'I'm sorry, Gozo, I just can't.'

'But I know where it is. I mean, I think I remember where I saw it. Let's just go there!' cried Gozo excitedly. 'Let's just go and find it. It'll be an adventure. It'll be . . .' Gozo stopped. Bartlett and Jacques were watching him. He knew that look. It was the kind of look people have when they're just waiting for you to finish before they tell you what *they've* decided to do. 'It'll be an adventure,' he mumbled unhappily. 'I *never* get to go on any adventures.'

Jacques le Grand grinned. Ever since Gozo had joined them, he always seemed to miss out on the really difficult, really exciting parts of their exploits. When they

20

had gone to get the splendid fruit called a melidrop for the Queen, he had missed the thrill and danger of the ice voyage. When they had gone to the City of Flames, after exploring the Margoulis Caverns, he had been locked up as a prisoner in the Pasha's palace, eating marzipan and cream all day, while Bartlett and Jacques were off discovering the underground city that no outsider had succeeded in finding before.

And soon, Gozo thought, they were going to take him back to his uncle Mordi, from whom he had run away, and he was never going to have an adventure at all!

'What about the river?' said Bartlett. 'Following the river will be exciting.'

Gozo shrugged dismissively.

'What about the Rift?' said Bartlett. 'How many people have been there?'

'That wasn't an *adventure*,' muttered Gozo. 'Nothing happened. We just . . . saw things.'

'And the Margoulis Caverns? You came with us to explore them.'

'We just saw things *there* as well!'

Bartlett grinned. 'Well, that's what it's like to be an explorer. You can't have adventures all the time. Sometimes things go smoothly. Most people are grateful when they do.'

'Well, I'm not grateful! I'm not!' cried Gozo. 'I want an adventure. At least *one*!'

'But Gozo, you don't get adventures by going to look for cities that don't exist. If an explorer believes every story he hears, he won't survive as an explorer long. Do you know who used to say that? Sutton Pu—'

'And do you know what *I* say?' demanded Gozo. 'If an explorer never listens to *any* of the stories he's told, he'll never discover anything!'

Bartlett and Jacques looked at each other in surprise. Gozo had a point!

'All right, Gozo,' said Bartlett eventually, 'you may be right. Sutton Pufrock may have been exaggerating. But you have to choose *which* story to believe. You hear this kind of story about every forest. Cities, kingdoms, treasure. We heard it about the Moray Jungle, and do you think we found anything there? Now, look. Look at that forest. Tell me: why should we believe it about this particular one?'

Gozo looked. The forest stretched to the horizon, dark, thick, deep. He remembered the thing that he had glimpsed the previous evening, the pale glint amongst the trees. Where was it now? He gazed, until the darkness of the trees filled his eyes, filled his mind.

'Why shouldn't you believe it, Mr Bartlett?' he murmured, hardly aware that he was even talking. 'Why shouldn't it be true about this one?' And then, as if the sound of his own voice had startled him, he suddenly turned around . . . to find Bartlett watching him closely, with a questioning, thoughtful look in his eyes.

Bartlett turned to Jacques. Very slightly, almost imperceptibly, Jacques shook his head.

'No, I don't know if it's true,' said Bartlett. 'It's probably just an old myth. But maybe it isn't. Maybe it isn't, Jacques. Maybe Gozo's right. How *do* we know?'

Jacques raised an eyebrow doubtfully.

'If an explorer never listens to any of the stories he's told . . .' said Bartlett.

The two explorers gazed at one another. Gozo hardly dared to breathe.

'Jacques, we'll never have another chance to find out.'

Jacques considered for a moment longer. Then slightly, almost imperceptibly, he nodded.

Bartlett grinned.

'Yes!' cried Gozo excitedly.

Jacques held up four fingers.

'A week,' said Bartlett.

Jacques shook his head.

'Five days,' said Bartlett.

Jacques thought for a moment. Then he nodded again

'Five days?' said Gozo.

'That's right,' said Bartlett. 'If we don't find whatever you saw in five days, we turn and head for the river, as we planned.'

'But Mr Bartlett, what happens if it takes six days, or seven, or . . .'

'Eight? Gozo, if you saw something from here, we'll be able to find it in five days. If we can't, then you didn't see anything.'

Gozo looked at the plain. He wasn't sure Bartlett was right. The forest was so vast . . . and thick . . .

'You have to set a limit, Gozo. In a forest like that, you can wander for weeks. You can wander so long you never make it out, like—' Bartlett stopped.

'Like Elwood Tucker? Is that what you were going to say?'

Bartlett nodded.

Gozo frowned for a moment. Then he jumped up.

'Let's go, then!' he cried. 'If we've only got five days, we'd better get started.'

The land fell away from the plateau in a series of sharp, rocky cliffs. Jacques led the way down. If anything, he was an even better climber than Bartlett, and going down can be more tricky than going up, as any climber knows. But Jacques' concentration was absolute. He was able to shut everything else out of his mind when he was engaged in a task, whether it was leading a camel through a sandstorm, or wading through a swamp, or swimming a river with his pack balanced on his head, or finding a way down jagged cliffs towards a plain thickly covered with trees . . .

But the forest didn't begin abruptly, as a wall of trees, as one might have imagined. At the foot of the last cliff the rock was cracked by wind and water, and there were only a few small bushes that grew out of the fissures. A stream trickled out of a pool in the ground and ran towards the plain. As the three explorers followed the stream, the bushes grew more numerous, and then the first trees began to appear, and eventually they were walking in and out of shadows thrown by branches above their heads, and the ground under their feet was carpeted with leaves and fallen twigs. But even here they weren't truly in the forest. The great density of trees waited ahead. Soon they would be in it.

Bartlett and Jacques stopped. They took off their packs and searched inside them. Eventually they each drew out a machete with a broad, gleaming blade.

Gozo stared at the blades. 'So this really *is* going to be an adventure,' he whispered.

'You can't get through a forest without one of these,' said Bartlett, and he tested the grip by tapping the back of the blade firmly against one of his boot heels. Jacques did the same.

'What about me?' said Gozo. 'I don't have one.'

Bartlett grinned. He looked up at the sun, while he could still see it, through the leaves above him.

'If the sun's there . . . then *that* would be north, where the river's flowing . . .' Bartlett put his left arm out, ' . . . and the thing that Gozo saw . . . would be *there*.' He swung his other arm around, with his machete, until it was pointing slightly to his right. 'Is that right, Gozo?'

Gozo frowned. 'I think so.'

Jacques motioned with his hand a little further across.

'Yes, that's right, Mr Bartlett,' said Gozo. 'A bit further that way.'

Bartlett adjusted his arm. Then he glanced at his two hands, memorising the angle between them.

'All right,' said Bartlett, dropping his arms.

'Are we ready?' demanded Gozo.

Bartlett nodded. 'One last thing, Gozo. Whatever happens: Perseverance. Once we go into that forest, there's no giving up, no matter how horrible it seems. We've set our limit, and we keep going until we reach it.'

'Give up?' cried Gozo. 'It's only a forest, Mr Bartlett! How horrible can it be? I've been in forests before, you know.'

Bartlett and Jacques exchanged a glance. 'Not like this one, Gozo,' said Bartlett. 'Believe me.'

Gozo put his hands on his hips. 'Really? Well, don't worry about Perseverance, Mr Bartlett. If we're going to have an adventure, we'll need Inventiveness and Desperation as well!'

Jacques le Grand raised an eyebrow. When they got into that forest, Perseverance from Gozo would be quite enough for him.

Bartlett laughed.

'There's nothing to laugh about,' cried Gozo. 'Just wait and see!' And before either Jacques or Bartlett could say another word, he set off in the lead, heading straight for the depth of the forest.

Gozo stopped. Neither Bartlett nor Jacques was

following him. 'Well?' he shouted. 'Aren't you coming? What about *your* Perseverance?'

'I'm sorry, Gozo,' said Bartlett. 'I was just thinking how much Inventiveness you were already showing.'

Gozo frowned. 'Why were you thinking that, Mr Bartlett?'

'Oh, just because . . . *that's* the direction we have to go in.' And Bartlett pointed his machete at a wide angle from the direction Gozo had taken.

Jacques le Grand couldn't stop himself laughing.

Gozo came back sheepishly.

'It's best to wait until everyone's ready, Gozo,' Bartlett advised him. 'That's what explorers do, you know.'

'Yes, Mr Bartlett.'

'Are you ready?'

'Yes, Mr Bartlett.'

'Jacques?'

Jacques le Grand nodded.

'Then let's begin,' said Bartlett. And he raised his machete, and Jacques raised his, and Gozo, who was standing between them, would have raised his, if only he'd had one, and together, side by side, they stepped forward and walked into the forest that lay beyond the Gircassian Rift.

4

If Gozo thought he knew what it was like to make his way through a forest like the one beyond the Gircassian Rift, it didn't take him long to see he was mistaken. He followed Bartlett and Jacques le Grand into the mass of the trees and almost at once they were in darkness. Overhead was an impenetrable matting of branch and vine. Dampness clung to the skin like a film, the air was chill, and the smell of decaying vegetation was heavy, a thick, sickly sweet odour that met you wherever you turned. And into this dark, cold, wet world came . . . noise! Somewhere high above was an endless screech and chatter. The noise didn't stop, not for a second. It waxed and waned, lulled you with a birdsong, then exploded with an ear-piercing shriek, got greater or less, but never ceased. Yet you never saw the animals that were screeching and hissing. You could only imagine what they were, parrots, monkeys, bats. Perhaps that made it worse. There was no warning, there was nothing to let you know when the next sound was going to burst out. Unseen, above you, was a world that was shrill with life.

But down here, in the shadows, it was as if nothing lived. It was as if you were moving in some kind of cavern beneath the living world, in a place that was the receptacle for things that had died, dead leaves and branches that had turned into a slippery, ankle-deep pulp under your feet, dead trunks which had crashed to the ground years before, and dead animals as well, probably, that had fallen out of the canopy.

Of course, if Gozo had stopped to look, once his eyes had become accustomed to the dim light, he would have found much that was alive. There were beetles, slugs, worms, fungus. If he had lifted up any rotting branch, dug under any trunk, he would have found a wriggling, squirming mass of creatures scurrying and crawling for cover. But he didn't stop to lift, or dig, and he hardly looked to see what was revealed beneath his feet as he kicked his way through the rotting leaves. He was too busy listening to the noise, and glancing apprehensively at the trees around him.

'You don't think there are any tigers here, do you, Mr Bartlett?' he said after a while.

Bartlett glanced back over his shoulder. He had just slashed through a low-hanging vine with his machete. 'Tigers? No, I don't think there'd be any tigers. What do you think, Jacques?'

Jacques shook his head.

'That's good,' said Gozo.

'Jaguars, I'd say, or pumas.'

'Jaguars?' whispered Gozo, almost too frightened to speak. 'Jaguars aren't—' He stopped, and winced, as a terrifying shriek pierced his ears from somewhere in the trees. 'Jaguars aren't like tigers, are they?'

'Not at *all*,' said Bartlett with effort, slashing at a branch. 'They don't have stripes, for a start.'

'And teeth?'

'Oh, yes. They've got teeth. What do you expect? I once knew a man who'd been mauled by a jaguar. Do you remember, Jacques? Pancho Nuñez. What did he lose again. His right leg? Or was it his left? You should hear the way he told the story, Gozo. First, the jaguar—'

Gozo stopped. 'Is this true, Mr Bartlett?'

Bartlett turned around. 'Of course it's true. Pancho was lucky. If you only lose a leg when a jaguar attacks, you've got off quite lightly, I'd say.'

'No, Mr Bartlett. Is it true there are jaguars here?'

Bartlett shrugged. 'Probably, Gozo. I'm only guessing, of course. But I'd say this kind of forest would be a place for jaguars. Tigers like a little more space between their trees.'

Gozo looked around at the dark trunks that rose on all sides.

Bartlett laughed. 'You won't see them like that, Gozo. If a jaguar attacks, it'll come from *above*.' Bartlett pointed his machete straight up into the trees.

Gozo looked up fearfully. A sudden bird's shriek made him jump. 'What colour will it be?'

'The jaguar? Black, probably,' said Bartlett.

'Black,' said Gozo. 'That would make it quite . . .'

'Hard to see? That's true, and you'd never hear them coming, either, not with all this noise.' Bartlett grinned. 'Don't worry, Gozo, we're too big for jaguars. They'd only come after us if they couldn't find anything else to eat.'

'They came after Pancho!' said Gozo.

'True, but Pancho's very small. Not much bigger than you, really.'

That didn't make Gozo feel much safer.

'Mr Bartlett, you're not making fun of me, are you?'

'No, Gozo. Stay close to Jacques and me. Jacques once fought off a puma single-handed. Did you know that?'

Gozo shook his head. He glanced at Jacques. But

Jacques was already moving again, hacking out a path with the sharp edge of his machete.

Jacques led for a while, and then Bartlett took his turn at the front. The one who was leading had to cut through the branches and vines that were in their way, and it was hard work. They advanced slowly. Leaves brushed at their faces and hanging loops of vine entangled them. The pulp of decaying leaves slipped and slid under their feet. They clambered over fallen tree trunks that were covered with moss and mould. Whatever gaps these fallen trees once left had long ago been filled, and the forest rose uninterrupted all around them. Screeches and shrieks continued to erupt above their heads. Gozo stayed close to Bartlett and Jacques, glancing upwards into the branches in case a black shape came leaping towards him.

Towards the end of the day they reached a stream. It was only a small stream, and there was no real gap in the forest, but the trees thinned a little along its course. In reality, the shadows here were still quite deep, but in comparison with the thicker part of the forest it was almost like being in broad sunlight. Here, for the first time, Gozo got a sense of the true height and majesty of the trees.

The dark space of the forest floor was the lowliest part. Above it, tree trunks soared towards the sky. Their branches were festooned with creepers, hanging like necklaces. Some had flowers. Some had fruits. Birds moved amongst the leaves. Some were dark, flitting shapes, others were breathtaking flashes of colour, reds, yellows, greens, blues. Gozo watched in awe, craning his neck. Suddenly there was a loud honking, and he saw a huge black bird rise out of a clump of branches, its wings flapping and brushing the leaves, spread as wide as the span of man's arms, its beak thick and curving like a horn.

Jacques had dropped his pack. He jumped across the stream and headed for a tree with yellow fruit hanging high in its branches. Bartlett and Gozo sat down and watched Jacques climb. Bartlett took out a couple of hard biscuits from his pack. These biscuits were as thick as your thumb and lasted for months, and like all explorers, Bartlett carried them to eat when there was nothing else to be found. He handed one to Gozo and kept the other for himself.

Gozo put the biscuit to his lips. The biscuits were

hard and dense, and he couldn't even bite them until he had softened them in his mouth. Jacques, on the other hand, was able to snap them with his hands. He could crush them in his fist, as well, to crumble them into hot water for biscuit soup, although Gozo didn't think this was a particularly important ability. Biscuit soup, in Gozo's opinion, wasn't much better than a dry biscuit, and a dry biscuit really wasn't that tasty either, but at least it filled you up.

Jacques climbed rapidly. Soon he was high in the tree.

'Looks like we'll be having dessert,' said Bartlett.

Gozo nodded.

'Should be nice,' said Bartlett.

'Yes,' said Gozo, but he wasn't really thinking about the fruit that Jacques might bring back. He was gazing in dismay at the forest floor on the other side of the stream, that dark, damp place beneath the lowest branches of the trees.

'Mr Bartlett,' said Gozo suddenly, 'I think we should stay beside the stream. It'll be easier if we do.'

Bartlett shrugged. 'Depends what direction the stream takes, Gozo. It may not go in the direction we need to follow.'

Gozo stared at the trickle of water in front of his feet. What was the chance it would go in the direction they wanted?

He was silent for a moment. 'You know, I can't be sure I really did see anything yesterday, Mr Bartlett, when I thought I did. It could have been a mistake. It could have been a . . . a . . .'

'A trick of the light?'

'Exactly. It could have been a trick of the light, couldn't it?'

'Well, we'll know in five days,' said Bartlett. 'If it was a trick of the light, we'll just find our way to the river and follow it to the sea, as we planned.'

'Five days . . . walking through *that*,' whispered Gozo, gazing across the stream.

Bartlett watched him .

'You know, I'm really *not* sure I saw anything, Mr Bartlett. And you don't want to listen to every story you hear, after all. You said yourself it was just an old myth. Couldn't we just . . . I mean, we could always just . . .'

This time, Bartlett didn't help Gozo finish his sentence. 'What, Gozo? What could we do?'

Gozo bit his lip. He stared sheepishly at his feet, avoiding Bartlett's eyes.

Bartlett waited a moment longer. 'Perseverance, Gozo.'

'I know, Mr Bartlett, but . . .' Gozo shook his head.

'You didn't have any trouble before, Gozo. Remember when they locked you in the Pasha's palace. You had Perseverance then. Weeks and weeks of it, remember?'

'The Pasha's palace! That wasn't like this forest. It was easy to have Perseverance there. I had as much marzipan as I could eat. I ate so much marzipan I got sick of it, and you don't know what that means. You don't know how much I loved marzipan before!'

'And the Margoulis Caverns? What about them, Gozo? We explored them for months, remember, before we ever got to the Pasha's palace. They were dark, darker than the forest. Sometimes they were cold and wet as well.'

'I know, Mr Bartlett. I know.' Gozo frowned. Somehow, the Margoulis Caverns weren't the same. They were dark, it was true, and sometimes cold, and often wet. But the Margoulis Caverns had been like a whole world in themselves, with soaring caverns studded with stalagmites and stalactites, and ledges of rock beside dark pools of water, and all the colours of the earth shimmering in the stone, gold, diamonds, blood-red iron, sky-blue sapphire, butter-yellow sulphur. You never knew what you were going to find next. The forest was nothing but darkness, and dampness, and the smell of decay, and branches scratching at your head, and vines slapping at your face, and noise exploding in your ears . . .

Bartlett smiled. 'Do you know what Sutton Pufrock used to say?' he asked quietly.

Gozo sighed. Sutton Pufrock again!

'He used to say: "If you start something and you realise it can't be finished—stop. If you start something and you just don't *want* to finish it—continue, or else you'll never finish anything again."'

Great, thought Gozo. It was easy for Sutton Pufrock. He was old now and rarely got out of bed. Not much chance that *he* was going to get stuck in some horrible dark forest with jaguars all over the place!

'And do you know what *I* say?' said Bartlett.

Gozo looked up.

'I say, the best adventures start when you least expect them. And if the only places you go are where you think you're *sure* to find an adventure, you'll probably never find one at all.'

'Really?' said Gozo.

'Yes,' said Bartlett. 'Perseverance, Gozo, it all starts with Perseverance. Right, Jacques?'

Jacques had returned while they were talking, his pockets bulging with fruits. He tossed one each to Bartlett and Gozo. They had a tough, bubbly outer skin.

'Some kind of custard pear?' said Bartlett.

Jacques nodded. 'Monkeys had eaten most of them,' he said.

Bartlett broke the skin of the fruit and tasted its flesh. 'Sweet. You're always good at picking the ripe ones, Jacques. '

Jacques smiled. He took a fruit for himself, broke it in half, neatly used the tip of his machete to scoop out the flesh, and began to eat it off the blade. Bartlett did the same.

Gozo was watching as if he expected them to roll over and die from poisoning in front of his eyes.

'Go on, Gozo,' said Bartlett, 'it's safe. How many dead monkeys can you see around here?'

Very gingerly, Gozo dug his finger through the bubbly skin of the fruit. The flesh was soft, pale and sweet. He pulled a spoon out of his pack and was soon eating hungrily.

'Did you get to the top?' Bartlett asked, reaching for another fruit. Jacques had taken the rest of the fruits out of his pockets and they lay in a pile on the ground.

Jacques nodded.

'See anything?'

Jacques shook his head. 'Not high enough. There were higher trees all around.'

'And the sun? Could you see where it was? Are we going in the right direction?'

Jacques shook his head again. 'Too far towards the north,' he said.

'Too far towards the north?' said Bartlett. 'That means we'll have to go . . .'

But before Bartlett said it, Jacques had already raised his arm. Gozo looked to see where he was pointing. Jacques' finger aimed straight across the stream, in a direction that would take them immediately back into the depth of the forest.

That was the direction they followed, the next day, and the day after that. And with each day that passed, wandering in that dark, cold, screechy world, Gozo became less hopeful, less certain that he had really seen anything at all from the plateau. Now it was Bartlett and Jacques who continued as if they didn't have a doubt. To be a great explorer, you have to be steady, not swinging from excitement to disappointment every moment like a monkey on a tree. This was something Gozo didn't yet understand, the meaning of real Perseverance. It meant that once you had decided what you were going to do, you did it with all your effort, as if you believed utterly you were going to succeed, as if you were certain to find what you were looking for. Anything less than this, and you were certain to fail.

And in fact, when he found the first trace of what they were looking for, Gozo didn't even realise it.

Four days had passed in the forest, and it was already the morning of the fifth. Once again they were hacking their way through the trees. Gozo's foot landed on something hard. It wasn't the first time Gozo had felt something hard beneath the slush of rotting leaves on the forest floor. There were logs and branches everywhere, slowly decomposing. So often had he stumbled over them, in fact, that Gozo had long ago ceased to pay attention when he felt one. He certainly didn't delay to glance down every time it happened, or stop to uncover the object underfoot. So why should he have stopped this time? And since he didn't stop, neither did Bartlett and Jacques le Grand, who were slashing through the forest in front of him.

But if Gozo *had* stopped to uncover the thing that he had felt, and if he *had* called out to the two explorers to come back and see what he uncovered, they would have found themselves looking at something that was certainly worthy of a moment's delay . . . if not more.

It was a piece of stone. It wasn't the size of the stone that would have made it so interesting to the explorers— it wasn't much more than a hand's breadth wide. And it wasn't the colour, a pale shade, almost white. It was the fact that, once they had uncovered it, and if they had used their machetes to free the stone from the soil around it, they would have found that its surfaces were perfectly smooth. And that its sides met at sharp corners. And that it was actually a rectangular block, with only one or two chips that had been knocked out of its edges. In a different place, of course, none of this would have been particularly remarkable. But the stone wasn't *in* a different place. It was lying on the floor of the forest beyond the Gircassian Rift. And as they uncovered it, as they freed it from the soil, Bartlett and Jacques, and maybe even Gozo, would immediately have seen that not nature alone, not wind nor water, not the pecking of birds nor the fists of monkeys, could have smoothed the surfaces and cut the corners of that block of stone. No, only human hands could have done it.

But they didn't stop, and they didn't uncover the stone and pry it out of the soil, and they didn't discover the smoothness of its sides and the sharpness of its corners. They continued into the forest. But the pressure of Gozo's foot had pushed away some of the leaves that covered it. And if only one of them had happened to throw a backward glance, if only for an instant, he would have seen a single corner of stone poking out of the slush, like a pale piece of bone embedded in the darkness of the forest floor.

5

In the afternoon, Bartlett, Jacques and Gozo stopped to rest on a log. Here the shadow was a little lighter, because the trunk on which they were sitting was newly fallen, and the trees that were growing on either side of it, thrusting up in a race for the sunlight, had not yet filled the gap that it had left in the canopy. Eventually, one of them would win the race, and throw a deep shadow over the forest floor, as before. The others, choked for light, would die.

Soon it would be the end of the fifth day. Gozo knew what that meant. But by now he was convinced that when he had thought he saw something from the plateau, it really had been just a trick of the light. Besides, after five days in the chill and noise of the forest floor, he was almost glad he'd been mistaken. What a horrible place for an adventure! Just imagine if they had to keep searching. And to think that he had tried to convince Bartlett and Jacques that five days might not be enough!

'We'll head for the river tomorrow morning,' said Bartlett.

Jacques nodded. He pulled a fruit out of his pack. 'We should build a raft,' he said.

'A raft?' yelped Gozo excitedly. 'I'd like to build a raft. If we build a raft we won't have to . . . to . . .'

'Walk?' said Bartlett.

'Exactly,' said Gozo, 'I would have said it if you'd given me a minute.' And he would have said a lot more. It wasn't simply walking that they wouldn't have to do, it was walking through this horrible, dark, wet, shrieking forest with a whole lot of jaguars just waiting to jump on top of your head.

'Of course, we'll have to watch out for alligators,' said Bartlett.

'Alligators?'

'In a river like that there are sure to be alligators.'

'That's not good news,' said Gozo. 'I don't suppose

Jacques ever killed an alligator single-handed?'

'I don't believe he's ever had the opportunity,' replied Bartlett.

Gozo frowned. He turned to Jacques. 'Would you like the opportunity?'

Jacques, chewing some fruit, thought about it. He shook his head.

'But if you did have the opportunity, you wouldn't just let it go, would you? You'd *take* the opportunity, right, Jacques?'

Jacques didn't reply. The expression on his face didn't suggest that he absolutely, *definitely* would take the opportunity, even if, for example, Gozo presented it himself.

'Well,' said Gozo, 'perhaps we should think about this raft idea a bit more before we make a decision.'

Bartlett grinned. He pulled out a fruit and ate it as well. They sat on the log for a while longer, and then they got up and started walking again. Soon they were back in dense, dark forest. Then they came to a tiny brook.

'We should stay near this, if we can,' Bartlett said. Gozo didn't understand why. 'Tomorrow,' explained Bartlett, 'we'll head for the river. If we follow this brook, we'll come to a stream, and if we follow the stream, we'll come to a creek, and if we follow the creek—'

'We'll come to the river!'

'Eventually, yes,' said Bartlett.

'And then we get to build the raft?' demanded Gozo, who'd been thinking about it ever since Jacques had mentioned it. That sounded like a real adventure, much better than looking for a city that didn't exist.

'Aren't you scared of the alligators any more?' said Bartlett.

'Alligators!' said Gozo. 'I'd like to *catch* one and *cook* it for dinner.'

They walked along the brook. After a few minutes Gozo stopped. 'Aren't we going the wrong way?' he said.

Bartlett and Jacques looked at him.

'Well, the water's flowing *that* way, so doesn't that mean the river's down there?'

'Yes,' said Bartlett.

'But we're going *this* way,' said Gozo.

'True.'

'Well . . . it's the wrong way, then.'

'Only if we're going to the river.'

Gozo shook his head in confusion. 'But you just said . . .'

'I said tomorrow, Gozo. Today, we're still looking for what you saw.'

'But I didn't see anything! I'm sure I didn't.'

'We said we'd give it five days. And if I'm not mistaken, today's still the fifth day. Right, Jacques?'

Jacques nodded his head gravely.

'You're not giving up, are you, Gozo? It doesn't matter if there's nothing to find, we'll finish what we started. Remember what Sutton Pufrock used to say.'

Gozo sighed. 'All right, Mr Bartlett. I remember. But I'm telling you, we're wasting our time.'

Bartlett grinned.

'We're wasting our time,' Gozo continued to grumble, as they moved off again. A little while later he stopped once more. 'Excuse me, Mr Bartlett. I've just got to . . . you know.' He disappeared into the trees.

Bartlett and Jacques waited.

'A raft, you think?' said Bartlett. 'It'll take us a couple of days. We'll have to get some logs and cut some vines.'

Jacques shrugged. Easily done in a forest like this!

'We'll need to be able to steer. And what about paddles? On the way back we'll need paddles to go against the current. Do you think there are waterfalls, Jacques? The plain's very flat . . .'

Jacques shook his head.

'No, I don't think so either. That's good.' Bartlett thought about it. Jacques was thinking as well, planning how they might build the raft, how many logs they would need, what kind of vines they could use. Suddenly Bartlett grinned. 'What *about* alligator for dinner, Jacques? Have you ever had it? We'll *have* to catch one.' Bartlett heard Gozo coming back. He raised his voice. 'We could use Gozo for bait. We just hang him over the edge of the raft, maybe just dangle his legs in the water—'

'*Mr Bartlett, what are you saying?*' cried Gozo at the top of his voice. A whole flock of birds took off amongst the trees, screeching madly.

'Nothing, Gozo. Why? What's wrong?'

'I heard you say something. I did! Something about bait.'

'Bait? Did I say something about bait, Jacques? *Wait.* That's what I said. How long will Gozo make us *wait*?'

Gozo crossed his arms. He gazed suspiciously at Bartlett and Jacques.

'Come on,' said Bartlett, 'we can't bait any longer.'

Jacques was laughing by now, he couldn't stop himself.

'All right!' said Gozo angrily, 'I know you're making fun of me. Just because I'm smaller than you, and a jaguar might want to eat me, and sometimes I can't—'

'Gozo, where's your pack?' said Bartlett

'See, you're making fun of me again!'

'No, really, where *is* your pack?'

Gozo frowned. He put his hands behind his back, as if to check whether it was still there.

'I must have . . . of course, I remember now!' Gozo smiled sheepishly. 'I leaned it against a wall and then I forgot to—' Gozo stopped. 'Mr Bartlett? Jacques? What's wrong?'

The two explorers were staring at him, eyes wide in disbelief.

'Mr Bartlett?' whispered Gozo.

'A wall?' said Bartlett. 'You said you leaned it against a *wall*.'

'A wall,' said Gozo. 'What's wrong with that? I just leaned it against . . .' Gozo stopped. Now *his* eyes went wide. 'Mr Bartlett! I leaned it against a *wall*!'

6

At first, they could see only a small patch of pale stone between the tree trunks. Gozo's pack was leaning against it. Then, as Bartlett and Jacques approached, they saw that the patch of stone was part of a wall, and the wall was part of a small, box-like building. It was partially ruined. The wall didn't rise much higher than Jacques' shoulder, and the roof was gone. A tree was growing in front of an opening, which must have been the doorway, and a larger, thick-trunked tree grew from the very centre of the house, with loops of vines falling from its branches.

'This isn't meant to be here, is it, Mr Bartlett?' said Gozo, as Bartlett stared at the house.

Bartlett shook his head. 'Not unless the myth is true.'

Jacques was already making his way around the out-side of the house, slashing a path with his machete. Bartlett put his hand on the wall and felt the stone. It was smooth. The individual stones of the wall had been care-fully cut with precise, straight edges that fitted evenly against one another. There didn't appear to be any mortar between them, and it was only the extreme accuracy of the stonecutters' workmanship that gave the wall its stability.

Bartlett squeezed behind the tree that grew in front of the doorway. Gozo followed him. They found that Jacques was already inside. The back wall of the building had collapsed entirely. At some time in the past, a tree had fallen and smashed through it. The tree had mostly rotted away, but a few pieces of worm-eaten wood still lay on the pile of toppled stones.

The floor of the house looked just like the rest of the forest, covered with the remains of past seasons of growth, a slush of rotting leaves, branches, fruits and cracked seed pods. Bartlett crouched and began to clear the slush away from a section of the floor. Beetles and centipedes swarmed away from his fingers. Underneath the slush he found soil, and he used the end of his machete to dig. Eventually the hole was so deep he could have put his arm in it up to the elbow. Jacques, who had been examining the inside of the walls, came over to look into it.

Bartlett shook his head. 'There's no stone here. The floor must have been made of earth.'

'No writing,' said Jacques. 'No pictures. No carving.'

'These people didn't know anything!' exclaimed Gozo.

Bartlett shook his head. 'Look at the walls, Gozo. Look at the way the stones are cut. It's as skilful as anything I've ever seen. Whoever built this place knew what they were doing.' Bartlett straightened up and turned to Jacques. 'Could be . . . what? Hundreds of years?'

Jacques shrugged.

'Impossible to tell,' said Bartlett. 'Fifty years, a hundred, five hundred.'

'Five hundred years!' yelped Gozo excitedly. Then he frowned. 'Mr Bartlett, five hundred years since *what*?'

'Five hundred years since this place was built.'

Gozo's eyes went wide again. He looked around the house, as if he were seeing it for the first time. 'Five hundred years . . .' he murmured. 'That's . . . that's . . .'

'Five centuries,' said Bartlett.

'Exactly!'

Bartlett was examining the stonework once more. Jacques knew what he was thinking, because he was thinking the same thing himself: people who are capable of building so well, of cutting stones so accurately and fitting them together with such precision, don't build just one tiny house with barely enough room to stand up in. For such people, a house like this would be an unimportant little building, probably the dwelling for a poor family, perhaps for the stonecutter himself. No, people like that are going to build a whole lot of other things . . . and most of them are going to be bigger and grander than this.

Yet in a forest of such thickness, they both realised, no matter how large and grand the building, you could walk straight past it if it were screened by the trees. An ancient temple might rise above the canopy only a stone's throw from where you passed, and yet you would have no clue that it was there. For how many days had they been wandering amongst hidden ruins? What, they started to wonder, had they already missed?

Bartlett and Jacques began to look at the trees around them. They had to get to the top of the forest, to the very top. They had to get high enough to see the forest over all the other trees, to scan it as an eagle scans it from the sky. But they weren't eagles, and the only way to get above the trees was on one of the trees themselves.

Which one was the highest? The trunks soared into the canopy, but how high did each one go once it disappeared into the matting of branches? Which one would rise above the others?

Bartlett and Jacques looked at one tree after the other. And in the end, they were both looking at the same one.

It was the tree that grew out of the floor of the house itself. Its trunk was enormous. Its branches began high up, as if it rose on a scale greater than all of those around it. The walls of the house, in some way, seemed to have protected it, to have given its trunk the space to grow and soar.

Bartlett didn't need to say anything. He glanced at Jacques, and Jacques nodded.

To climb the tree was to rise out of one world and into another. Gozo followed Jacques and Bartlett up the trunk. At the bottom was the shadowy, damp world of the forest floor. But with each moment that passed, as he hauled himself up from one branch to another, every-thing was becoming lighter, the smells fresher. Leaves began to look green, not black. And so many greens! Bright greens, light greens, drab greens and dark greens. And the noises became louder. Birds screeched close by. They flitted out of the leaves, around your shoulders, above your head, below your feet! This was their world, here, and you had entered it from below.

Gozo heard a series of giggling shrieks. He turned to see a band of monkeys scamper along a branch and leap off into the air, one after another, disappearing amongst the leaves of another tree, golden-coloured monkeys with dark faces and white beards, and it all happened so quickly he couldn't be certain that he really *had* seen them, but he must have, because he had never seen golden-coloured monkeys with black faces and white beards before, so his imagination wouldn't have just made it up. And it wouldn't have made up the image of the monkey at the back of the line stopping for half a fraction of a second, and turning his head, and grinning at him, either, would it?

Suddenly the world was light and brisk and Gozo felt light and brisk as well. He almost felt he could fly like the birds around him. The ground had disappeared. The floor was made of leaves.

But climbing the tree wasn't easy. It wasn't like climbing a tree in the orchard of his uncle Mordi's farm. Branches from other trees jutted across, coiling vines tried to snag him. The density of the forest made it hard to climb into the air, just as it made it difficult to walk along the ground.

Bartlett and Jacques were above him. Gozo soon lost track of height. He must be very high, he knew, high enough to be frightened if he had been able to see the ground when he looked down. But beneath him there were only branches and leaves. What would happen, he wondered, if he fell? Would he land softly in a nest of leaves? Would he plunge through them and plummet to the ground? He looked up to see if the two explorers were near the top, but all he could see was Bartlett's weathered boots pushing off from a branch above his head. Jacques must be even further up. Gozo's arms were starting to ache and his wrists were tiring. But he kept going. If it was Perseverance that was needed, he wasn't going to fail! He wasn't going to miss out on this. He wasn't going to miss getting to the top and seeing whatever Jacques and Bartlett were going to see.

He didn't. The tree, as Jacques and Bartlett had guessed, was taller than any of those around it. That afternoon, the eagles soaring above the plain, hanging in the air and training their sharp eyes on the forest below them, saw three heads, one after another, break through the leaves at the top of the canopy. And with the sunlight shining full on their faces, and with the branches on which they stood swaying in the breeze, first Jacques le Grand, then Bartlett, then Gozo, looked out over the forest, which spread beneath them like a noisy green sea.

Everywhere they looked, there were birds, erupting out of the trees, gliding above them, dipping and dropping again.

But it wasn't the birds that seized their attention. After a moment, they hardly noticed them at all.

Not far away, the green sea of the forest was interrupted.

One after the other, Jacques, Bartlett and Gozo saw it. One after the other, they stared.

A huge white building rose out of the trees. It was circular, and narrowed as it rose, like a cone, with a series of broad ledges running around it. At the back of each ledge was a row of dark doorways. Each ledge had fewer doorways than the one below, and at the top only one doorway was visible.

'What is it, Mr Bartlett?'

Bartlett didn't reply.

There were more buildings in the distance. They lay scattered across the forest like knucklebones. Not all of them were like the big cone that was nearest, some were square, some were flatter. Even far, far away, Gozo could see the tip of a building.

'There are so many, Mr Bartlett! There's one, two, three, four, five, six—'

Suddenly Gozo heard Jacques' voice, low, urgent. '*Look!*'

Gozo glanced at Jacques. Something had caught his eye. Whatever it was that Jacques had spotted, he was now gazing at it with intense concentration. So was Bartlett.

Gozo felt a wave of apprehension. Slowly, almost reluctantly, he looked to see what they were watching.

Below them, on one of the ledges of the big conical building, outside one of the doorways, a human figure had appeared.

7

The eagles that soared above the Gircassian Rift, that floated on the breezes over the plain beyond, knew the truth about what lay within the forest. They had known the truth for centuries.

What the eagles saw, what they knew, was that far out in the dark sea of the forest there were islands where trees did not grow. These islands were white, and had dark holes in them, and from high in the air they appeared as the scattered skull and bones of some gigantic animal that had fallen and crashed millions of years before. Over time, the sea of the forest had washed over the smaller islands and submerged them, trees had grown and covered them from view. But the larger ones remained exposed, the forest sea lapped at their edges, unable to claim them. Here, lizards sometimes darted out into the sunlight, huge green lizards with bellies as thick as a man's arm, and an eagle, flying over the plain, might swoop towards one, and if it were lucky, might rise, the dark shadow of the lizard wriggling in its talons, and fly towards the sun. And sometimes, as the sun set, the stark whiteness of one of these islands might catch the rays at a certain angle and glint for a moment, transmitting the secret of its existence, just for that moment, even to those whose eyes weren't as sharp as an eagle's.

Yet how many people, over the centuries, had happened to be standing exactly in the right place, at the right time—on the plateau above the forest, for instance, at sunset—to see this? Gozo was perhaps the first. This is what Gozo had seen, the sun's rays reflected from far off in the heart of the forest. The reflection came from so far away that he wasn't able to see any detail, just the flash, just a fleeting glint of light that caught the eye only because everything else around it was dark. And it lasted only a moment, before the angle of the sun's rays shifted and the glint was gone.

The islands that the eagles saw in the sea of the forest, the bones that lay scattered across the land like the skeleton of a gigantic beast, were buildings. The whiteness that glinted in the setting sun was stone. As year followed year, as the forest went through its unending cycle of growth and regrowth, as trees grew, thickened, flowered, seeded and eventually died, crashing to the forest floor amongst the thin trunks of saplings already pressing upwards to replace them, the buildings remained.

The rumours and stories that were told about the great forest beyond the Gircassian Rift contained, like an oyster, a grain of truth over which layer upon layer had been fabricated. Sometimes the human imagination finds it hardest to imagine that things are, in reality, simple. It prefers to create great myths, construct scenes of impossible richness, paint images of incredible heroism, than to imagine that the people in times past were similar to those who live today. It prefers to turn a house into a palace, to replace its wooden roof with silver, to fill its storerooms with gold, when, in reality, the most amazing thing is not the amount of gold that a house contained, or the richness of its construction, but . . . the mere fact that there was once a house at all.

In the forest beyond the Gircassian Rift there had once been many small houses. Most were now submerged under the forest. Falling trunks had smashed them, growing roots had toppled them. There had been some larger houses, as well, that one might have called palaces, although they were never filled with gold, and their roofs, which had mostly caved in and disappeared, had been cut from the wood of the surrounding trees. And there had even been larger structures, which one might have called temples, in which the people who made these buildings worshipped the beings who, they believed, created the forest and all that was in it. These were the buildings that the trees had been unable to cover up, and which the eagles saw as they soared above the forest.

Where did the stone for the buildings come from? This was a mystery, as so much about this place was a mystery. The forest contained no rock. It grew upon lush soil, and with every year that passed the falling leaves and branches added to the soil's thickness. Perhaps the rock had been cut from the cliffs near the Gircassian Rift. Perhaps it had been quarried at the coast. For some reason, the people who constructed the city had brought it far into the forest, to the places where they chose to build. They must have felled many trees merely to create the track along which they dragged the rock that they had cut. Once, this track must have stretched through the forest like the wound from a knife, just as the Gircassian Rift sliced through the desert plateau. But the forest had long ago regrown, and there was no trace of this track, except perhaps a few ancient, rotting tree stumps still standing in the darkness of the forest floor, and a few pieces of stone, dropped and forgotten where they fell.

What had happened to these people? There was one story that told of a great flood, but since the story contained much that was false, there was no reason to suppose that this particular part was true. What the human mind does not know, the imagination creates. Perhaps, in reality, there had not been a flood, but a drought. Perhaps an earthquake. Perhaps a plague. Perhaps other people had arrived on the coast in ships, and conquered the people in the jungle, killed them, and in turn had died, unaccustomed to the forest and incapable of surviving in it. How many possibilities there were! Perhaps, buried somewhere under the leaves that had covered so much in the years that had passed, there was a clue to the story. A wall in one of the buildings with some writing on it, possibly, or, if these people did not have writing, a picture. Would any people allow itself to disappear without leaving some trace, some last echo to say 'This is what happened'?

And if, amongst these ruins, people still lived, where had they come from? Had they survived the destruction of their city, or arrived later? This, not even the eagles knew.

8

'Do you really think we should be doing this?' said Gozo.

Bartlett didn't respond. Neither did Jacques. They were hacking furiously with their machetes. Leaves flew, branches splintered.

Gozo tried again. 'Mr Bartlett, should we be doing this? Are you sure?'

'Doing *what*?' demanded Bartlett, wincing with effort as he swung his machete and slashed through a branch.

'This!' cried Gozo. 'Going there . . . without even stopping to think.'

'*Think*?' Bartlett slashed again.

Jacques slashed as well. It was all Gozo could do to keep up with them as they lopped a path through the trees. And the real problem was, Gozo didn't know if he wanted to keep up. Those old buildings, to tell the truth, had looked a bit scary, and he wasn't at all certain what kind of people would live in them, or what they would be inclined to do to other people who arrived out of the forest. Besides, no one would have spotted the three explorers while they were up there in the tree, he was almost certain. It would have been the easiest thing in the world to slip back to the brook, and follow it to a stream, and follow the stream to a creek, and follow the creek to the river . . . without giving the least disturbance to anybody.

'What about the raft we were going to build?'

'What *raft*?' demanded Bartlett. 'Can you remember *anything* . . . about a *raft* . . . *Jacques*?'

Jacques didn't bother to reply. His machete flew.

'But what if—'

'What if *what*?'

'What if they're cannibals or something, Mr Bartlett?'

Now Bartlett stopped. He turned to Gozo. He laughed. 'You wanted an adventure, Gozo. Here it is!'

Gozo glanced at Jacques. He had the same look in his eyes as Bartlett, a gleam of excitement, impatience. It was the look of explorers who know that a new adventure is about to begin. There was no stopping them now, Gozo could see it.

They paused for only an instant. Then they were advancing again, hacking through the branches and vines that hung in their way.

And then they came to a halt.

They were at the edge of the trees. Before them was the cone-shaped building they had seen when they climbed to the top of the forest. It rose above them, with its great ledges and row upon row of blank, empty doorways.

There was a clear area around the building. It was bright with sunlight. Gozo glanced backwards for a moment, at the darkness of the forest floor behind him. Never, he thought, could he have imagined that he would find himself thinking of those trees as somewhere safe, somewhere from which he wouldn't wish to come out. But after five days in the forest, at least he knew what to expect there. For most people, the familiar, no matter how unpleasant, is preferable to the unknown. At

this moment, Gozo was experiencing the true test of the explorer, the moment when he faces the unknown—the unexpected, the unpredictable, something that perhaps will be dangerous—and must choose to go on.

'You don't want to turn around now, do you, Gozo?' said Bartlett.

Gozo looked up at Bartlett. He hesitated for a moment. Then he frowned with determination, and shook his head.

'Good,' said Bartlett, and he glanced at Jacques, his eyes alight with anticipation, 'because neither do we!'

Where was the person they had seen from the tree? The building loomed above them. Its wall curved away to either side. It was perfectly smooth, built with the same precision as the walls of the house they had first discovered. They could see no way in.

They began to walk around it.

Bartlett stopped. He frowned in concentration. 'Can you hear something?' he whispered.

They all listened. They heard birds, of course, from the forest. Their noise was shrill and piercing. But that wasn't what Bartlett meant. There was something else as well, something they hadn't heard in the forest before. You could hear it when the sound of the birds grew fainter for a moment. And once you had heard it, and began to listen for it, you realised it was in the background all the time, rising and falling in its own rhythm.

'Isn't there some . . . some kind of . . .'

'Music?' said Bartlett softly.

'Yes,' whispered Gozo. 'I would have said it if you'd given me a minute. 'It's like . . .'

'What, Gozo?'

'It's like . . . a flute.'

Bartlett nodded. They stood and listened to it. The music of the flute, or whatever instrument it was, wavered in the air, strange, sweet but sorrowful, and Gozo didn't know what to make of it. He had never heard anything like it before. They crept forward quietly. The sound grew louder.

Then they came to a large gap in the wall, and they found that they were standing at the foot of a long stairway. It was broad at the bottom, but narrowed as it climbed, like the building itself. It was like the building's spine, and the ledges that came off it were its ribs. The stairway ended at the very last doorway at the top. A few of its stones were missing, and there were one or two bushes growing in the gaps, but it was mostly intact. It must have been a magnificent sight, this long, straight stairway reaching up to the heights, three or four or five or however many centuries ago, when the stones were newly polished and without defect.

The music continued. They could hear it clearly now, although they still couldn't see where it was coming from. It was as if the music beckoned them. They began to climb the stairs.

At the second level of the building they saw someone sitting on the stone in front of a doorway. The person's back was turned towards them. They could see the end of the wooden flute or pipe from which the music came.

The music stopped. The person looked around. Two soft brown eyes gazed at them.

Suddenly Bartlett realised that he was still holding his machete. He placed it carefully on the stone. He held out his hands to show that they held no weapon, and that he meant no harm.

The musician, still sitting, swivelled around to face them.

'Good morning. My name is Bartlett, and this is Jacques le Grand,' said Bartlett. Jacques laid his machete down and nodded in greeting. 'And this,' continued Bartlett, 'is Gozo.'

Gozo didn't do anything. Not a sound, not a movement.

'Gozo!' whispered Bartlett.

But still Gozo made no move. He was frozen on the spot, staring at the person who had been playing the flute.

She was a girl, no older than he. She was the most beautiful girl Gozo had ever seen.

'Well, don't worry about him, he's just doing his imitation of a rock,' said Bartlett, and he grinned, and he elbowed Gozo smartly in the ribs.

Gozo jumped. The girl, who had been watching him, broke into a smile.

Gozo flushed red. He flushed so red that he found

himself wishing, for the *second* time that afternoon, that he could just run off into the forest and hide himself under the trees.

The girl led them along a path beneath the forest canopy. Here, the branches and slush had been cleared away, and the ground was a track of beaten earth. She walked swiftly, nimbly following the ribbon of earth between the trees. Once, when she came across a branch that had fallen onto the path, she stopped to lift it and toss it into the forest.

She was small, no bigger than Gozo. She carried her flute. Her clothes were simple, light-coloured trousers and a tunic made of material woven from some kind of fibre, cotton or something similar. On one of her wrists was a bracelet of finely plaited leather, to which was attached a small piece of polished emerald in the shape of some kind of bird. She had a leather braid tying her long brown hair at the back. She wore no shoes, and Bartlett, marching directly behind her, could see her strong, slender ankles, and the way her feet slid onto the earth, almost as if her toes were reaching for it, to feel and grasp it.

Not once had she spoken. After Bartlett's introductions, she had simply stood up, walked past them, and gone down the stairs, quite calmly, not as if she were frightened, or even surprised to see three strange people appear out of the forest, but with perfect confidence. When she got to the bottom of the stairs, she had turned to see if they were

64

following, and when they came down to join her, she set off along the path.

Soon they saw another building ahead of them, framed by the trees. Eventually they reached it. Before the building was a small open area of grass. The girl pointed at the ground, looked meaningfully at Bartlett, and then pointed at the ground again. Bartlett nodded, to show that he understood. She walked away. She stopped after a few paces, looked back to see that they were waiting where she had shown them, and then disappeared round the corner of the building.

This building was unlike the other one. It was flatter and broader. There were two levels, both block-like and rectangular. The lower level rose to about twice the height of a man, and above it, set back from the edge so that it stood on a kind of platform, was the upper part of the structure. Its wall was blank, and as far as they could see, it had no door. In fact, from where they were standing, there was no obvious way into the building at the lower level either. But Bartlett and Jacques didn't go to find the entrance. They stayed exactly where the girl had left them, silently examining the building from where they stood.

'Mr Bartlett! We're not just going to wait here, are we?'

Bartlett grinned. 'I see you've got your voice back, Gozo.'

'I never lost it. I just . . . I just . . .'

'Forgot how to use it?'

'No!' said Gozo indignantly. 'I just thought maybe it wasn't the best time to speak . . . back then . . .'

'You mean when I asked you to? Of course, that would be a terrible time to speak.'

Bartlett and Jacques laughed.

'It isn't funny!' said Gozo.

'Of course not,' said Bartlett. 'It isn't funny at all.'

But Gozo wasn't convinced they didn't think it was funny, at least, not funny *at all*, because they were still grinning, so obviously something was amusing them. He wished they didn't have to keep standing there, doing nothing, just where the girl had left them. Bartlett normally wasn't one to stand around.

'Mr Bartlett,' said Gozo eventually, 'can't we at least go to see what's happening?'

Bartlett shook his head. 'That would be unwise, Gozo. We've been asked to wait. That's what we'll do.'

They did. Whatever the girl had gone to do, it was taking a long time. Gozo was beginning to wonder if she hadn't forgotten about them, or just left them there as a joke, when suddenly, there was a noise above them.

Gozo looked up. The girl had reappeared on the upper level. Behind her, where there had been—he was *certain*—no doorway before, there now appeared to be something that looked very much like a doorway indeed, quite a large doorway, in fact, with a man coming out of it.

The girl sat down on the edge of the platform with her legs dangling over the stone, looking down at the three newcomers. But they were all staring at the man who was coming out of the doorway, even Gozo, who might easily have frozen once more under the girl's gaze, if not

for the fact that the man behind her was easily the largest
. . . heaviest . . . *fattest* man that Gozo had ever seen. In
fact, until he saw this man, Gozo couldn't have imagined
that any human being could be so big. The man wore
a huge robe, like a smock, and it billowed over his enormous belly. His chin, his whole jaw, was lost in folds of
flesh, and his eyes were like tiny sultanas almost buried
between his eyebrows and his bulging cheeks.

The man shuffled towards the edge of the platform.
Each step, as he grimaced with effort to raise his foot
and swing it fractionally forwards, was a moment of
danger, as his enormous body teetered and rocked and
threatened to fall.

It must have taken him five minutes to reach the edge
of the platform. He had to stop for breath between each
step. And all the time the girl looked down, watching the
strangers' reactions.

As the man advanced, a second man had come out
from the doorway behind him. He was as tall as the first
man, but lean, and completely bald. When the first man
finally came to a halt, with a loud, exhausted grunt, the
other man was standing beside him.

There was silence. The large man was still breathing
heavily. The other man was looking at Bartlett. He
scrutinised him closely. Then he examined Jacques.

Bartlett and Jacques didn't know who was waiting
for whom, whether the bald man was waiting for the
fat man to recover, or whether the fat man was waiting
for the bald man to begin . . . or whether they were
both waiting for something else entirely. Still no one said

anything. Just as Bartlett thought he might have to start the introductions, the bald man spoke.

'This is the Falla of Run,' he said, putting out his hand towards the man in the billowing smock. 'Run, in case you don't know it, is where you are.'

Bartlett nodded graciously.

'I am Bartlett. And this—'

'I know who this is,' said the second man. 'This is Jacques le Grand, isn't it?'

'It is,' said Bartlett. He glanced at the girl. Obviously she could talk, after all.

'And this one, who is this?' said the man.

'Gozo,' said Bartlett. He frowned. Why didn't the man know Gozo's name, if the girl had told him who they were?

Bartlett looked at the Falla. He loomed above them on the platform, rocking a little, as if his legs would not carry his enormous weight much longer. If he tumbled from where he stood, Bartlett thought, he'd fall on them! The other man ought to take him back inside, or at least bring him a chair. But the bald man seemed to be in no hurry to do anything. He was still watching Bartlett closely, inquisitively, as if he expected something of him. Bartlett had the feeling that something was going on, but he didn't know what.

Suddenly the other man shook his head. 'You don't know me, do you, *Bartlett*?'

Bartlett frowned. The way the man had said his name, *Bartlett*, wasn't the way you would speak to a perfect stranger. There was a tone of amusement in it, mockery.

'Know you?' said Bartlett. 'Should I know you?'

'Oh yes, I think you should,' said the man. 'If someone had asked you, I bet you would have said you'd recognise me in an instant. I bet you would too, Jacques.' The man turned to Jacques for a moment. 'But look at you both,' he said, shaking his head in a show of disappointment. 'When the moment finally arrives, well . . . you don't recognise me at all!'

Bartlett and Jacques exchanged a disbelieving glance. All at once they knew who it was, they *knew*, even though it was scarcely possible that it was true.

Only Gozo didn't know. But perhaps, when he saw the look of astonished recognition on Bartlett's face, even he understood.

Bartlett looked back up at the platform.

'Well?' said the man.

'You . . . You've lost your hair,' said Bartlett.

'True. I lost it all one day, just like that. Overnight. It just fell out. It's funny what happens in life, isn't it? Me losing my hair . . . You turning up here.'

It's funny what happens in life? *In life?*

'But Elwood,' said Bartlett, 'you're meant to be dead!'

9

'I don't know who built these places,' said Elwood Tucker. He waved a hand towards a building that loomed up out of the trees on their left. 'No one knows. Must be hundreds of years old, maybe a thousand. The people who built them are long gone.'

Elwood Tucker kept walking. They had left the building where they had seen the Falla. In fact, they hadn't spoken to the Falla at all. Elwood Tucker had disappeared from the platform and the next thing they knew he was standing beside them, and then he was leading them away. Soon they were on a path under the trees, following him in single file, and every time Bartlett tried to ask Elwood Tucker what he was doing there, and what had happened to him, and how he had survived when everyone thought he was dead, and any one of the other hundred questions that came into his mind, Elwood simply ignored his query. Now they were walking alongside an area that had been cleared of trees, and it was covered with long vines of ripening pumpkins. The pumpkins were enormous, bulging, fat.

'Look at this,' said Elwood, as they walked along the edge of the field. 'Have you ever seen anything like it? The soil is rich. And there aren't any diseases. The plants here are the healthiest you'll ever see. They produce twice as much as you'll get anywhere else.' He glanced over his shoulder at Bartlett. 'Have you got any food, by the way?'

'Biscuits,' said Bartlett. 'Plenty of biscuit.'

'Thought so. You didn't look like you were hungry.' Elwood Tucker shook his head. 'Explorers' biscuits. I remember those. Haven't had one for ten years, and I can't say I miss them.'

'We got fruit from the forest as well.'

'You'll find fruit here like you've never seen before, Bartlett.'

'Melidrops?' called Gozo from the end of the line.

'Melidrops? You want melidrops? Who needs them? You'll have other fruit here instead.'

'We brought one to the Queen!' exclaimed Gozo. 'No one else could have done it.'

Tucker laughed derisively. 'So that's what you're up to now, is it, Bartlett? Getting melidrops for queens?'

'They had to go on an ice voyage to do it!' cried Gozo. 'It was the *bravest* voyage ever. Tell him, Mr Bartlett.'

'Really, Bartlett? The *bravest* voyage ever?'

Bartlett didn't reply. He could hear Elwood Tucker laughing to himself.

They turned from one path onto another, and then another again. Eventually they came to a square building. Here Elwood Tucker stopped.

'This is where you can stay,' he said.

'Here?' said Bartlett.

Tucker nodded. Bartlett, Jacques and Gozo went in to have a look. The building had a doorway but no windows. The roof was made of wood. The walls were constructed out of very precise, careful stonework. The house that Gozo found in the forest must have looked like this before it was ruined, except this one was a bit larger, and there was one other difference: in the middle of the floor was an enormous circular stone.

Tucker was waiting for them outside.

'It's very nice,' said Bartlett, when they came out again.

Elwood Tucker nodded.

'Do you put all your guests here?'

Tucker didn't reply. He arched an eyebrow. There was a hardness in Elwood Tucker's eyes, Gozo had begun to notice, and sometimes it was visible and sometimes it was hidden.

'Shouldn't we meet the Falla?' said Bartlett.

'You've met him,' said Tucker.

Bartlett grinned. 'Should we meet him *properly*, Elwood?'

Tucker stared at Bartlett as if he didn't understand. He glanced at Jacques le Grand for an instant.

'Seriously,' said Bartlett. 'Doesn't he want to talk to us? Doesn't he want to know why we've come here?'

'*Why* you've come here?' said Elwood. 'Aren't you an explorer, Bartlett? And you, Jacques? Isn't that why you're here? To *explore*?' He peered inquisitively at Jacques and Bartlett for a moment. Then he jabbed a finger in Gozo's direction. 'What about him? Where did you find that one?'

'I'm learning to be an explorer!' declared Gozo, putting his hands squarely on his hips.

'Learning, is he? So you've taken over from Sutton Pufrock, have you, Bartlett? He couldn't be much older than you were when Pufrock got hold of you.'

Jacques frowned. *Got hold* of him?

'Or you, Elwood,' said Bartlett quietly.

Elwood Tucker's gaze became very hard. Then he sneered. 'So what is it, Bartlett? Why *are* you here? *Not* to explore? I can't believe you've changed. Not you.'

'No,' said Bartlett, 'I haven't changed. Neither has Jacques. You're right, we're here to explore.' He paused. 'And you, Elwood? Why are *you* here? You still haven't told us.'

Elwood Tucker was silent. He eyed Bartlett coldly. The two men faced one another. Tucker was the taller, Bartlett the stringlier. Without knowing precisely what it was, Gozo had the sense that there was something very powerful, strong and intense between them . . . and now, at last, it couldn't be ignored.

Seconds passed. The strain grew. Finally Elwood's eyes shifted. He glanced at Jacques for an instant. When he spoke, there was no warmth in his voice.

'Well, I suppose I discovered I wasn't as great an explorer as I thought. Not as great as *you*, Bartlett. I got lost in the forest. If I'd tried to get out, I would have got lost again.'

'And so you stayed? For ten *years*? You just stayed? You didn't—'

'What?' demanded Elwood Tucker. 'Didn't what? Have you ever starved in a forest, Bartlett? You with your *biscuits*. Have you ever dug up the root of a tree with your fingernails to see if you could eat it? Have you ever been lying on your back and seen fruit hanging from the branches above you and been too weak to climb and get them? Do you know what that's like?'

Bartlett shook his head.

'Well, perhaps you should find out before you ask any more questions!' Elwood Tucker stared at him for a moment longer. 'I'm going now,' he said. 'I've got things to do.'

'When will we see the Falla?' asked Bartlett.

'The Falla? Don't worry about him. I've told him all about you. He'll meet you when he's ready.'

'And when will he be ready?'

'No, things are different here, Bartlett. People aren't in a hurry. Time moves slowly in Run.' Now Elwood Tucker smiled. When he spoke again, his voice was different, soothing. 'Enjoy yourselves. Rest. Spend a few days with us before you leave. I'll send someone with

74

food. Soon you'll see how we live here.' He began to walk away, but turned back after a couple of paces. 'They call this place Run,' he said, 'but I don't know why. Me, I call it the Forest of Plenty.'

And Elwood Tucker turned once more, went to the path, and disappeared under the trees.

Bartlett and Jacques were deep in thought. Gozo looked around the clearing, then scrutinised the house behind them for a moment. He turned back to the two explorers, wondering what was going on.

They glanced at one another. Jacques le Grand answered the question in Bartlett's eyes with a shake of the head. Jacques had never really liked Elwood Tucker. Like everyone else, he admitted that Elwood had the makings of a great explorer, but he had never really felt he could trust him. Too arrogant. Too sure of himself.

'People change, Jacques,' said Bartlett. 'It happens.'

Jacques raised an eyebrow sceptically.

'How do you know?' Bartlett said. 'If you almost starved to death in a forest, maybe you'd change as well.'

'You believe that?' said Jacques.

'He lost his hair!'

Jacques shrugged. People lost their hair—it didn't mean they'd gone digging up roots with their fingernails.

'He must have been through something,' said Bartlett.

'Grandpa Simmit lost his hair,' said Gozo. 'He lost it all after Grandma Zole broke her leg.'

'You see, Jacques?'

'But he was very old.'

Jacques rolled his eyes. He turned to Bartlett and said, in a low voice: 'Not as great as *you*, Bartlett!'

'Is that it?' said Bartlett. 'You doubt him because he said that?'

Jacques nodded. He could remember how great had been the rivalry between Bartlett and Elwood Tucker, how they had vied to prove themselves to Sutton Pufrock. It was legendary amongst explorers. To say that Bartlett had been better than him . . . that was the last thing Elwood Tucker would admit. A man could change, it was true, but could a man change that much?

'*Couldn't* he have changed?' said Bartlett. He stared out along the forest path that Elwood Tucker had taken, as if the answer to his question might be out there, even if Elwood himself had disappeared long before. 'Why not?' he murmured. 'It's possible, isn't it?'

10

The Falla was reclining on a couch carved from wood and generously padded with cushions. One end of the couch was higher than the other, to support the great weight of the Falla's shoulders and head. Elwood Tucker sat opposite on another couch. The Falla reached out for a bowl of sweets that had been placed on a small table beside him. His thick fingers scrabbled at the table for a moment, searching out the bowl, and when they found it, they took a handful of the sweets and transferred them directly to his mouth. Not once did he look at what he was doing. All the time, his eyes remained fixed on the ex-explorer.

The room was bright, but there were no windows. The light came from three oval openings in the roof. Through the openings, the blue sky was visible. Only a bird would have known that anyone was inside.

In addition to the Falla and the ex-explorer, there was a third person in the room. The girl with the flute was sitting on the floor at the Falla's feet, with her back against his couch. She was watching the ex-explorer as well. Elwood Tucker would have preferred not to have her in the room, listening to what he was saying, but if the Falla allowed her to stay, there was nothing he could do. She was the Falla's daughter, and her father knew no greater delight than to have her near him, unless it was to have her near him *and* playing her flute. Tucker hated that flute, and would have been more than happy if the girl had never played it again in her life. No one had taught her what to do with it, and she just seemed to make up her own music, which was very strange music, as it seemed to him, aimless, incomprehensible, disturbing. It made him wonder what was going on in her mind.

He was telling the Falla what he had done with the new arrivals. The Falla nodded, as he listened, chewing his sweets. Then he interrupted, and turned to the girl, holding out a handful of sweets in his fleshy palm. She shook her head. The Falla grimaced. 'You should eat, Anya,' he said.

Anya shrugged.

The Falla gazed at her with a look of great concern. His daughter was slim, ate sparingly, and was not as fat as he would have liked her to be. He was always trying to feed her things, and she was always refusing.

If only he would try less, Elwood Tucker sometimes thought, she might eat a little more.

The Falla turned back to the ex-explorer. 'So, you left them in the Circle House? Is that what you said?'

Elwood Tucker nodded. He looked closely at the Falla, waiting to see what he would say. The Circle House was small, but it was no ordinary building. Long ago, before he grew too fat to walk, the Falla himself had shown it to him. In all of Run, only the Falla and Elwood knew its secret.

But the Falla merely said: 'That's a long way.'

'Not too far,' replied Tucker, wondering whether the Falla had heard him properly. 'It's not too far to the Circle House.'

'Perhaps I've forgotten. I haven't been there for a long time.'

You haven't been *anywhere* for a long time, thought Tucker. The Falla was so large, and his hips were so unsteady and painful when bearing the great weight of his body, that it had become impossible for him even to get down the stairs to go outside. His walk to the edge of the platform that afternoon was the longest journey he had taken in years.

'You're my eyes and ears, Elwood,' said the Falla. 'My eyes and ears.'

Elwood Tucker nodded.

'But you can't hide anything from me,' he said sharply. 'You know that, don't you, Elwood? I'd know if you did.'

'Of course you would, Falla.'

'That's right!' said the Falla, and he reached for another handful of sweets.

Elwood Tucker glanced at the girl. She was watching him with narrowed eyes. Sometimes, from the way she looked at him, Elwood got the feeling she didn't like him at all. Not that you could be sure. She hardly ever spoke, which was another eerie thing about her, as eerie as the strange music she was always making up.

'You say they came from a ship?' said the Falla.

Elwood turned back to the Falla. 'No. I said they came from the other side of the forest.'

'And the other side of the forest is . . .' said the Falla, waving a hand to prompt the ex-explorer.

'Desert.'

'Yes. And desert is . . .' he said. 'Tell Anya.'

'Empty earth, dry, without trees,' said Tucker impatiently, glancing at the girl.

'Empty earth, dry, without trees,' repeated the Falla solemnly, waving a finger in the air, for Anya's benefit. 'No one comes to Run from the desert, Anya. No one except Elwood and these others. They are like him. Isn't that so, Elwood?'

'Yes,' said Tucker. 'They are like me. I knew them before.'

'Yes. That's what you said. You knew them before. Were they your friends?'

Tucker nodded.

'Even the little one? He must have been your friend when he was a baby!'

Anya grinned. Tucker noticed it out of the corner of his eye. He really wished the Falla would make her leave.

'I didn't know the little one, Falla.'

'You see? I *knew* you didn't know him. There's no use trying to hide anything from me, Elwood. I always find out.'

'Of course, Falla.'

'But you knew the other two?'

'Yes. And they are like me.'

'Well, that's good. You're such a help to me, Elwood. It will be better to have three of you than only one.'

Tucker didn't reply.

'The Circle House is such a long way away,' said the Falla suddenly. 'Perhaps you should bring them closer.'

The ex-explorer gazed closely at the Falla, trying to understand exactly what he meant by that. But the Falla's eyes, half buried in the folds of his face, gave no hint.

'It's not so far,' said Tucker carefully.

The Falla was silent. Tucker waited.

'Perhaps I should see them.'

'Why, Falla? Why trouble yourself?'

'To see why they've come here.'

'They're explorers, Falla. They came to explore, just like me.'

'But what if they want to leave?'

Tucker laughed. 'Leave? Where will they go? Into the forest? No one can survive there. If they hadn't found us, they'd already be dead. Didn't you see them? They were starving.'

'Starving? Were they starving?'

'They'd been digging up roots to see if they could eat them. They told me.'

The Falla frowned. 'Are you sure? They didn't seem . . . Starving?'

'You didn't see them up close, Falla. They were like skeletons. Just like I was. Do you remember when I came here, Falla? I was starving. I was almost crazy.'

'Were you starving, Elwood? I can't remember.'

'I was a skeleton, Falla. You must remember. I'd been digging up roots with my fingernails.'

'Like your friends?'

'Exactly.'

The Falla took more sweets and munched them thoughtfully. It was a long time since Tucker had arrived, ten years. If Elwood said he had been starving, that's how it must have been. A man wouldn't forget whether he had been starving or not. It was something that would live in his memory forever.

Elwood Tucker glanced at Anya. The girl was watching him impassively.

'You're a great help to me, Elwood,' said the Falla eventually. 'I don't know what I'd do without you. I've become a little too large for my own good, I think.'

'Only a *little*, Falla.'

The Falla smiled. His eyes disappeared completely inside his face. Elwood Tucker smiled as well.

'So you're looking after them?' said Falla.

'Of course,' replied Tucker.

'You've given them food?'

'I've sent Pfister.'

'Pfister? Pfister's a little . . .'

'Pfister's all right,' said Elwood Tucker. 'He does exactly what I tell him.'

'All right.' The Falla nodded. 'I'll leave it to you. And I don't need to see them, you say? Not yet?'

'There's no rush,' said Elwood. 'You can see them later.'

'Yes, later.'

'There'll be plenty of time.'

'Plenty of time. They're not going anywhere, are they, Elwood?'

'No, Falla. They're not going anywhere.'

The Falla smiled contentedly. He rolled over on his back. Elwood Tucker got up to leave. The Falla was going to sleep. After his journey onto the platform, it would probably take him the rest of the day to recover.

The ex-explorer glanced at the girl. She was still sitting at the foot of the couch, her eyes fixed expressionlessly on his face.

As he left, he heard the sound of her flute start up in the room behind him.

11

Pfister was a tall young man. His long
arms dangled out of his tunic, which
was too short for him at the wrists.
His neck was long as well, and very
skinny, and the Adam's apple in
his throat bobbled up and down
whenever he spoke or swallowed.
He appeared on the path, coming
towards the Circle House with an
enormous basket. There were corn
cakes in the basket, and pumpkin
tarts, and roasted legs of turkey, and
pastries and nuts and fruit, and jugs
of a sweet drink that would make
you drowsy if you drank enough of it. When he reached
the house he unpacked it all in front of the explorers.

According to Pfister, the people living in Run now
weren't the descendants of the ones who had built the
city. Who *they* were, no one had any idea. They had disappeared without leaving any clue behind them, not a
trace, except for strange carvings that could be seen on
some of the buildings, which no one understood.

'So where *did* you come from?' asked Bartlett, licking
his fingers before selecting a second turkey leg to eat.

'Ships,' said Pfister, biting into a turkey leg as well. He
had joined in with them as soon as they started eating.

'*Apparently* we came from ships. Everyone, that is, except Elwood Tucker, who came from the desert. But he's special, and *apparently* no one else ever did that.'

Pfister said *apparently* a lot, because he himself had been born in Run, and there were many things he had never seen, but only heard of. For instance, he didn't know what a ship was. '*Apparently* it's something that floats on the sea,' he said. But he didn't really know what the sea was, either. '*Apparently* it's a huge amount of water.'

'And what's a desert?' asked Bartlett, without telling Pfister where they had been before arriving in Run.

'A desert, *apparently*, is a place where there aren't any trees,' said Pfister, and then he gave Bartlett a sceptical look, as if he didn't quite believe it. No trees? How could someone who had been born in the forest, who had spent every day of his life surrounded by trees, believe that there was a place where no trees existed?

Gozo shook his head in amazement, and took another mouthful of the sweet drink that Pfister had brought. Even *he* knew more than Pfister!

The story, as far as Bartlett could extract it from the thin young man, was that *apparently* the people in Run had come, over the years, as survivors from shipwrecks on the coast. The coast, as Bartlett knew, was uninhabited, and these must have been ships that had been blown off course in the ocean. Those who survived the shipwrecks would scramble ashore, only to find an impenetrable forest in front of them. According to Pfister, some would eventually realise that they were never going to be rescued

85

by sea, and would decide to try to cross the forest. Most died in the attempt. One or two, sometimes, if they were lucky, would survive in the forest long enough to stumble into Run, and that was how their lives were saved. Here they would stay. *Apparently* that's what happened, said Pfister, although he himself had been born in the forest, as he had said, and so had his parents, and it was his grandparents or even his great-grandparents who had, at different times, survived various shipwrecks and the forest journey to arrive in Run.

By the time Pfister had told them all this—because he wasn't the kind of person who kept exactly to the point, and was easily sidetracked, and wanted to ask lots of questions about the things he *apparently* had been told—they had finished their meal, and were all feeling very full and satisfied. Gozo, for one, was quite drowsy as well. It was weeks since they had eaten food like that, since before they had set off for the Gircassian Rift. Jacques alone had accounted for four big turkey drumsticks and more corn cakes than he could count—or at least he had stopped counting, because Pfister had brought so many corn cakes that there didn't seem much point in counting them anyway.

By now it was dark. Pfister left them. That night, in the Circle House, they slept soundly, without disturbance, just as three explorers should sleep who have arrived after two weeks in a canyon and five days in a forest. And when they awoke the next morning, Pfister was already there again, waiting for them.

This time Pfister had a bag with him. It was empty, and hung from a long strap around his shoulder. 'I'm meant to take you wherever you want,' he said. 'Elwood Tucker told me to show you whatever you want to see.'

'Where *is* Elwood?' said Bartlett.

'Oh, I don't know. He's busy. He's always busy.' Pfister looked down at the bag, as if he were trying to make up his mind about something. 'I'm meant to get some quinces,' he said. 'But I can get quinces any time. I could get them tomorrow, for example, if you'd prefer. Or you could come with me now.'

Bartlett glanced at Jacques. A slight smile crept across Jacques' lips.

'Of course you don't want to go picking quinces!' said Pfister. 'Why should you? I'll get them tomorrow.'

'No,' said Bartlett, 'if you have to get them today . . .'

'No, I'll get them tomorrow.'

'No, really.'

'No, I'll get them tomorrow. That's what I said yesterday, by the way, so it won't be the first time.'

'I bet it's not the second time, either,' said Bartlett.

'No, it isn't,' said Pfister, looking at Bartlett in surprise. 'How did you know?'

'Just a guess,' said Bartlett.

Pfister nodded. 'That was a very good guess. I wish I could guess like that.'

'So do I,' said Gozo.

'Well, we should go,' said Bartlett.

'Yes,' said Pfister. 'Where to?'

'Wherever you want to take us.'

Pfister thought. 'I'd better go to the bakers,' he said, 'to tell them they won't be getting any quinces. They're the ones who are expecting them, you see. I should have gone to tell them yesterday as well.'

'But you didn't?' said Bartlett.

Pfister stared at Bartlett once again. This stranger really *did* know how to guess things.

Pfister took them along the path they had followed the previous day, but then he turned onto another path, and another, and gradually, as he led them towards the bakery, they began to get a sense of what Run was like. They went past a field of ripening maize. Bartlett asked Pfister to stop and then they went out amongst the stalks. After all the time they had spent in the dark world of the forest floor, it was wonderful to feel the sun again, to stand in a field and not see the shadow of a tree on the ground, to feel the breeze running over your face and hear it rustling the corn. It seemed hardly believable that in only a few minutes, if they walked back into the forest and left the track, they would be back in that world, that it still surrounded them, and it would take days and days of walking to get out of it.

Bartlett broke off an ear of corn and peeled back the leaves, and the kernels of maize gleamed yellow, full and heavy.

'Look at this corn,' he said with admiration, holding out the cob.

'That? That's not even ripe yet,' said Pfister. 'Give it another couple of weeks.'

Bartlett glanced at Jacques. 'Elwood was right,' he murmured, 'this really is a forest of plenty.'

Later they came to a field where the plants sprouted cotton-like tufts of white fibre. The fields in Run occurred suddenly, like big holes that had opened in the forest. Then they went back to the path, and soon they saw a house, and there was a woman sitting on the roof, cooking over a fire. She smiled at them, and waved as they walked past. They waved back, although Gozo thought it was very strange to see someone cooking on a roof, and wondered whether there was some reason she couldn't come down.

Next they came to a pond. When they looked in from the edge, they could see hundreds of fish darting in the water. The fish, *apparently*, had originally been brought from streams in the forest. They bred in the pool. Then Pfister took them back onto the path and they soon came to a long, flat building, from which they could hear a strange shrieking noise. The door of the building was closed, but there was a small slit in the wall beside it. Pfister hoisted Gozo up so he could see.

'Turkeys!' cried Gozo excitedly.

Bartlett and Jacques looked in as well. The building was half covered with the remains of a roof that had collapsed, and it was full of forest turkeys. Huge, strutting, they fanned their wings, kicked out their feet, squabbled and gobbled at each other in uproar.

'If you want one, you just go in and take one,' said Pfister. He grinned. 'But it's not so easy to catch them.'

'I'd take a turkey every day!' exclaimed Gozo.

'No, you wouldn't,' said Pfister.

'I would so. I love turkey, you've got no idea. We only have it twice a year at home, and I eat as much as I can.'

'But if you could have it every day,' said Pfister, 'you wouldn't want it so much. You might want something else.'

Gozo frowned.

'He's right,' said Bartlett. 'When you're at home, and you can have as many melidrops as you want, how many do you have?'

'That's not the same, Mr Bartlett! At home, melidrops aren't special. They're everywhere. They're not like turkeys.'

'How many do you have?' repeated Bartlett.

'One or two . . . sometimes . . .'

'See? But Jacques has as many as he can get, because he hardly ever gets to eat them. Right, Jacques?'

Jacques nodded.

'What's a melidrop?' asked Pfister.

'Just a fruit,' said Gozo.

'Listen to yourself, Gozo,' said Bartlett. '*Just a fruit*. It's the sweetest, most delicious fruit there is.'

'Mr Bartlett, you don't even like them!' cried Gozo.

'True. They're a bit too sweet and delicious for me.'

'We had to get one for the Queen,' explained Gozo, 'and Bartlett and Jacques went on an ice voyage to do it.'

'I see,' said Pfister, more confused than ever. 'Is that what you were doing when you got shipwrecked?'

'We didn't get shipwrecked,' said Bartlett.

'But how did you get here?'

'From the desert.'

Pfister looked at him in disbelief. 'Like Elwood Tucker?'

Bartlett nodded.

Pfister fell silent. He led them away from the turkey house. But he didn't say anything now, thinking about what Bartlett had just told him.

The bakery turned out to be a simple square building, with a row of ovens at the back, shelves at the sides and a big kneading table in the middle. On the shelves were rows of corn breads and cakes.

The two bakers were standing amongst sacks of flour. They didn't look happy with Pfister.

'This is Bartlett and Jacques and Gozo,' said Pfister.

'Hello,' they said. Then they turned back to Pfister. 'Where are our quinces, Pfister?' demanded one of them.

'I'll get them tomorrow, I promise,' said Pfister.

'That's what you said yesterday.'

'Is it?'

'Pfister, we need quinces. Do you hear? How can we make quince cakes without them?'

Pfister reached up to the shelves and started filling his bag with cakes. The bakers watched him discontentedly.

'Go on, take some,' said Pfister.

'Just like that?' said Gozo.

'Of course. What do you think they're here for?'

Bartlett took a cake. Jacques took a couple. Gozo grabbed half a dozen.

'Don't take more than you can eat,' said Pfister. 'There's always more.'

'What about you?' demanded Gozo. 'You've filled your whole bag!'

'These aren't just for me, Gozo.'

'Who are they for?'

'You'll see.'

The bakers had already gone back to work at their kneading table, only glancing around occasionally to glare at Pfister and mutter angrily to each other under their breath.

'Maybe you really should get them some quinces,' said Bartlett as they left. 'Don't worry about us. We can look after ourselves.'

'Oh, they're always after quinces,' replied Pfister. 'They've got a month's supply, but that doesn't stop them worrying.'

'But you promised you'd get them yesterday.'

'Now I promised I'd get them tomorrow. That's just as good,' said Pfister.

'Where are we going?' asked Gozo, munching on a cake.

'Grandma Myrtle. I promised to visit her.'

12

'So, you really didn't come from a shipwreck?' Pfister muttered as he led the way from the bakery. He took a cake out of his bag and nibbled it, and then he pulled another one out and offered it to Bartlett, who had already finished the one he had taken from the bakery.

Bartlett shook his head, but Jacques reached forward and took it instead.

'I told you, Pfister, we came from the desert,' said Bartlett. 'Just like Elwood Tucker.'

'What's it like, really, the desert?'

'It's just like you said. There aren't any trees. There's hardly anything at all.'

Pfister thought about this. 'What about birds? Are there birds?'

'Barely a single one.'

'Monkeys?'

Bartlett shook his head.

'What *is* there, then?'

Bartlett stopped. He squatted down and tapped his finger on the bare earth of the path. 'Nothing, Pfister. Nothing but the earth itself.'

Pfister glanced at Jacques, and then at Gozo.

'It's true,' said Gozo. 'There was hardly anything there at all.'

Pfister stared at him for a moment longer. Then, as if looking at Gozo had just reminded him of something, he slapped his forehead. 'I know what I promised to do! Come with me. You'll love this, Gozo.'

'I thought you promised to visit your Grandma Myrtle,' said Bartlett.

'I promised that as well!' Pfister cried over his shoulder. He was already walking again.

Bartlett shook his head, and glanced at Jacques, who grinned. There seemed to be no end of things that Pfister promised to do, and it hardly seemed to worry him when he carried them out, as long as he completed them eventually. But perhaps, thought Bartlett, that was the way things worked in Run, where time moved slowly, as Elwood Tucker had said.

Pfister was speeding along on his long, thin legs, and they all had to hurry to keep up. Gozo was running. Soon Pfister took a turn. They began to hear shouting. As they kept going, the shouts got louder. The path ended. They were at the edge of a large clearing. The ground rose in front of them, and they couldn't see what was beyond the crest. But it was from there that the shouts were coming.

They walked to the top of the crest. Beneath them was a huge rectangular pit, far deeper even than the height of Jacques le Grand. From end to end would have been a good long sprint. The walls were lined with white stone and the floor was grass. In each of the pit's four corners was something that looked like a horn carved out of stone, standing upright with its mouth curving forward. And at the middle of each side of the rectangle was a set of stairs that led down to the bottom.

But Pfister didn't lead them down. Below them, in the

pit, six boys were running, shouting and chasing, all trying to get hold of a small leather ball. Opposite them, on the bank above the other side of the pit, a seventh boy was sitting and watching.

One of the players had got hold of the ball. Two others were waving and calling out to him, darting around and trying to slip away from their opponents so he could throw to them. Another boy tried to block the throw. The one who was holding the ball was big, with a very athletic build. Suddenly, he twisted, lunged, and threw the ball towards a teammate. The pass was good but the other boy fumbled and suddenly the ball was free again and his opponent squeezed past him and quickly slapped it against the wall and sent it bouncing towards the horn in the opposite corner of the court. Now everyone swung around and two boys sprinted and one of them dived ahead to seize the ball, and then he was up and running towards the horn with the other one at his heels and the most amazing thing, in all this flurry and action, was that . . . none of the players once made contact with another.

'You have to get the ball in the horn,' said Gozo.

Pfister nodded. He was watching the game with interest. The ball had just been thrown but it had missed the horn and now another player seized it as it came off the back wall. He was running. An opponent came at him from the front. Just as they were about to collide, they both stopped. They faced off, breathing heavily. The boy who had the ball was very small. He was close to the wall, and a second opponent rushed in to trap him, waving his hands in his face.

'Side Ball,' muttered Pfister to himself. 'Come on, Muss, Side Ball!'

But the small boy called Muss didn't hear him, or ignored him if he did. He continued to bob around on the spot, trying to find an opening through his opponents' arms.

'Want to play?' said Pfister to Gozo.

'They don't seem to need an extra player.'

'Oh, don't worry about that. They're playing threes. They can easily play fours. Bertram over there's just waiting for someone else to turn up.'

'Well,' said Gozo doubtfully, 'they look like they know how to play very well, and I—'

'Know how to play very well?' muttered Pfister, as Muss continued to search for an opening. 'This is ridiculous. What's wrong with these boys?' Suddenly he shouted: 'Throw or Give!'

The boys all looked up, realising for the first time that someone had arrived.

'Throw or Give!' repeated Pfister. The small boy with the ball searched for an opening in desperation.

'Too late,' shouted Pfister. 'Give!'

'Oh, Pfister!' said one of the small boy's teammates.

'Oh, Pfister *what*? How long does he think he can hold it? Throw it here, Muss.'

The small boy reluctantly threw the ball to Pfister.

'Where have you been, Pfister?' said one of the boys who had been cornering Muss. 'You promised you'd come to train us.'

'I was busy,' said Pfister. 'I had to get quinces for the bakers.'

'That's what you said *yesterday*!' cried another of the boys.

'Be quiet, Gandel. I saw that throw of yours just now and it was awful. If you can't do better than that, there's no point trying to train you anyway.'

Gandel hung his head. Gozo didn't know what Pfister was talking about. Gandel was the big boy who had thrown the pass that another boy had fumbled. It wasn't Gandel's fault that his teammate had dropped it. If he had to play, decided Gozo, he'd definitely want to be on Gandel's side.

'Now,' said Pfister, still holding the ball, 'this is Gozo. He comes from the desert, where I bet they *really* know how to play WallBall. Looking at him, I'd say you should watch out for his forward angle throw.'

The boys all looked up at Gozo. Gozo frowned. His *forward angle throw*?

Pfister prodded him. Bertram, who had been watching from the other side, was already on his way down to join the game.

'But Pfister, I really don't think—'

'Go on, Gozo,' said Pfister, nudging him down the stairs. 'I'm sure our rules are the same as the ones you use in the desert.'

'But Pfister! I've never even *seen* this—'

Pfister wasn't listening. He just kept pushing Gozo down to the court, while calling out: 'Muss, when you're finished, bring him back to the Circle House.'

'Oh, Pfister,' said Muss, 'all the way out to the Circle House!'

Pfister held out the ball. 'You're not going to argue, are you?'

Muss shook his head. Pfister tossed the ball to him.

By now Gozo was at the bottom of the stairs, standing on the grass of the court. 'Mr Bartlett!' he cried, 'you're not going, are you? Jacques? What about you? You're not going to leave me here!'

But Pfister was already on his way back up the stairs, and a moment later Bartlett and Jacques were walking away with him.

'*Mr Bartlett? . . . Jacques?*'

'He'll be all right, won't he?' said Bartlett, when Gozo's screams had become quite faint behind them.

'Of course he will,' said Pfister. 'You know what Wall-Ball's like. No one ever gets hurt. Not badly, anyway . . . I mean, not often.'

As he walked, Pfister was pondering the desert again. It intrigued and puzzled him. The notion that someone else could come from there, someone other than Elwood

Tucker, was an amazing discovery. For so long he had been told that only Elwood came from the desert, it had almost started to seem that the desert was Elwood's private domain.

'We knew him, you know,' said Bartlett.

'You *knew* Elwood Tucker?' repeated Pfister incredulously.

Bartlett nodded. 'Before he came here. He was a friend of ours, right, Jacques?'

Jacques shrugged. Perhaps not exactly a friend.

'He was an explorer, Pfister, just like us. He went everywhere. He was always looking for something new. No mountain was too steep nor any desert too wide to stop Elwood Tucker.'

None of this meant anything to Pfister. He had never seen a mountain, and a desert, as Bartlett had already discovered, was a purely theoretical notion for him.

But this didn't sound like the Elwood Tucker that Pfister knew. 'Elwood Tucker says this is the best place in the world. He says he never wants to go anywhere else, and neither should we.'

'That's what he says *now*, Pfister. That's not the way he used to talk.'

Pfister shook his head. 'No, all of the time before he came here, wherever he went, he says, he was only looking for Run.'

Jacques raised an eyebrow. But Bartlett shook his head. People could change. And when they changed, it was natural they'd talk about the past in a way that changed as well.

Suddenly Jacques spoke. 'What does Elwood *do*, Pfister?'

Pfister shrugged. 'He helps the Falla.'

'How?'

Pfister didn't reply.

'Tell us about the Falla,' said Bartlett.

Pfister didn't reply to that, either. Suddenly he began striding out with all the speed in his long, thin legs. If he went any faster, he'd be running.

Bartlett threw a questioning glance at Jacques, and they both increased their pace to keep up.

Then the tall conical building was ahead of them, where they had arrived the previous day.

'Is that where we're going?' said Bartlett.

'Yes,' said Pfister. 'The HoneyCone.'

Now they could hear music coming from the direction of the building.

'When we were here yesterday there was a girl playing some kind of flute,' said Bartlett.

'That's Anya,' replied Pfister. 'She's often here. Grandma Myrtle likes her music.'

They stopped to listen. The music was strange, sweet but sorrowful, just as it had been on the previous day.

'Come on,' said Pfister suddenly. 'Grandma Myrtle will love to meet you. She's not like me, you know. She wasn't born in Run.' He frowned. 'She knows all kinds of things.'

13

Anya was sitting on the stone of the HoneyCone, exactly where Bartlett and Jacques had found her the previous day. As they climbed the stairs, she turned to watch them.

She beckoned to Pfister. Pfister went over and crouched down beside her.

Anya whispered something in his ear.

'Playing WallBall,' said Pfister.

Anya whispered something else.

'Oh yes, I'm sure he's played before. Gozo's played WallBall before, hasn't he, Bartlett?' he called out.

Bartlett shook his head.

Anya's eyes went wide, and then she glared at Pfister. You didn't need to hear any words to know what she was thinking!

'Oh, don't worry, Muss'll look after him,' Pfister said to her. And that was all they saw of Anya, because Pfister then took them inside to see Grandma Myrtle, and when they came out again, Anya had disappeared.

Grandma Myrtle was sitting at a loom. She sat straight-backed, her arms outstretched, and her fingers were strong, nimble and elegant.

'Is that you, Anya?' she said, without taking her eyes off the loom. 'Are you tired of playing?'

'It's Pfister, Grandma Myrtle. I brought you cakes.'

'Thank you, Pfister. Stay out of the light, please,' said Grandma Myrtle. Still she didn't turn to glance at the

door, but continued working. 'That's better,' she said, as Pfister moved aside from the doorway. Behind him, Bartlett and Jacques moved aside as well. Grandma Myrtle's fingers flitted rapidly, tirelessly. 'And the cotton, Pfister? Did you bring the cotton?'

'Oh, no!' cried Pfister, slapping his forehead.

'Pfister, you've forgotten, haven't you?'

'No, Grandma, I just . . .'

'What, Pfister? What's your excuse this time?'

'I brought you something else instead,' said Pfister hurriedly. 'Much better than cotton. Two new people, Grandma!'

Now, for the first time, Grandma Myrtle looked

around, although her fingers continued to pluck at the loom. A second later she turned back and went on working, gazing in concentration until she had finished whatever it was she wanted to finish. Only then did she drop her arms and turn to her visitors once more.

'Welcome,' she said.

'This is Bartlett, Grandma Myrtle. And this is Jacques le Grand.'

'Hello,' said Bartlett. Jacques nodded.

'Thank you for being so patient,' said Grandma Myrtle. 'If I stop in the middle, everything gets ruined.'

'I understand,' said Bartlett.

'They arrived yesterday,' said Pfister. 'They're staying in the Circle House.'

'Only yesterday?' said Grandma Myrtle. 'You look well, both of you. Did you come from a shipwreck?'

'No, we came across the desert,' said Bartlett.

'Like Elwood Tucker?'

'Yes.'

'Ah . . .' Grandma Myrtle nodded, and she gazed at the two explorers more closely.

'They knew him, Grandma! They knew him before he came here.'

'Really?' said Grandma Myrtle. She was silent for a time, still peering at her visitors. Suddenly she spoke again. '*I* was in a desert once. Let me remember its name. Madbor . . . Medber . . . Midbar . . .'

'Modbir,' said Bartlett. 'That would be the Modbir Desert.'

'You're right. That was it, the Modbir Desert.'

'Grandma,' cried Pfister, 'you were in a desert? You never told me that.'

'What's the point? You're never going to see one, Pfister, and be thankful you're not. An empty place, horrible. Anyway, I wasn't really in it. I just saw it. We called in at a port . . . What was it called? . . .'

'Gavingar?' said Bartlett

'That's it. It was on the journey that ended when we were shipwrecked off this coast, Bartlett. The ship called in at the port for a couple of days to get supplies, and we went for a drive to the edge of the town, my husband and I, that is. This was so long ago, I can't remember the details. We hired a carriage for the day, I do remember that. The town was at the edge of the desert, and all we could see was sand and rock, and far off in the distance, a small clump of trees.'

'That would have been the Dharmit Oasis.'

'Would it? We didn't go there, we just glimpsed it from the edge of the town. It looked so small, as if you could have put it on the palm of your hand and carried it away.'

'We've drunk at the Dharmit Oasis, haven't we, Jacques?'

Jacques nodded. 'Very pure water,' he said.

'It's a shame you never got to try it, Grandma Myrtle,' said Bartlett.

Grandma Myrtle shrugged. Pfister had sat down on the floor, and was gazing at her and Bartlett in turn as each of them spoke, trying to imagine the places they were describing.

'I'd love to see that,' he murmured.

'Nonsense, Pfister!' said Grandma Myrtle. 'You'd hate the desert. A boy like you, brought up in the forest, you wouldn't know where to begin. Now, where are these cakes of yours? Aren't you going to offer any to our friends?'

Pfister jumped to his feet. He grabbed a couple of cakes out of his bag and handed them to Bartlett and Jacques, and then he took the others and placed them on a wooden plate, on a small table that stood beside Grandma Myrtle's loom.

'Take one for yourself, Pfister,' said Grandma Myrtle.

Pfister darted back and took one. He sat down on the floor again. Bartlett and Jacques sat down as well. Grandma Myrtle turned further towards them in her seat, and to do it, she used her arms to swivel her body around. Only now did Bartlett and Jacques see that her two legs were useless, withered by disease, and they realised that she probably couldn't walk.

Bartlett looked around the room. Tapestries covered the walls. They were very beautiful, and skilfully made, but they all showed the same subject, a certain kind of bird. It had a yellow beak, tiny red feathers on its head, and a pattern of red, yellow and black feathers on its body. Some of the tapestries showed it flying, some perched, some pecking at a fruit, some nesting. They showed it from the front, from the side, and from all kinds of other angles. It appeared in every one of them, and when Bartlett looked back at the loom, he saw that the unfinished work showed what would become yet another image of the bird, with wings stretched, legs extended, at the moment of taking off into the air from a branch.

'It's a kind of hummingbird,' said Grandma Myrtle. 'We call it the Lou-Lou.'

'They nest at the top of the HoneyCone,' added Pfister. 'You should see them at dusk. The air's full of them.'

'And you like to weave tapestries of them?' said Bartlett.

Grandma Myrtle smiled. 'Sometimes, I think the Lou-Lou is the most perfect of nature's creations. I would like, just once, to achieve that perfection.'

Bartlett nodded and looked around the room once more. Jacques, who was still staring at the tapestries, nodded thoughtfully as well.

And as they looked at the tapestries, Grandma Myrtle watched the two explorers with a thoughtful gaze, just as she had watched them when Bartlett told her that they had known Elwood Tucker before he ever came to Run.

14

'Don't you have *any* rules in the desert?' demanded Gandel, picking himself up off the ground and stopping the game.

'Well, in the desert we . . . we . . .' mumbled Gozo.

'We *what*? You're dangerous, playing like that.'

'I'm sorry. I just . . .'

'You've never played WallBall, have you?' said Gandel suddenly. 'You've never played it at all!'

Gozo shook his head. His secret was out. He was surprised it had taken so long, all of a minute, during which he had bumped into two people, knocked over another, and finally tripped up Gandel as he ran towards the goal, all the time without once getting near the ball.

'Pfister!' muttered Gandel to himself.

'Don't you play it in the desert?' said another boy, whose name was Hardy.

'I've been through the desert, but I'm not *from* there. I don't know *what* they do in the desert.'

The boys stood around, wondering what to do. Gandel seemed to be the leader. He had picked up the ball and was tossing it from hand to hand.

'Maybe you should just watch first,' he said.

Gozo thought that was a very good idea.

'Muss, you can explain everything to him.'

'Why *me*?' said Muss. 'Why can't—'

'Pfister told you to look after him, that's why.'

'He told me to take him back to the Circle House when we were finished. That's all he said.'

'Go on, Muss,' said Gandel, and the others said it as well, and eventually Muss began to trudge towards the edge of the court, taking Gozo with him.

'I'm sorry,' Gozo whispered to Muss, as they walked up the stairs. 'I didn't mean to stop you playing.'

They sat down on the grass ridge overlooking the court. The game began again.

'Do you really come from the desert?' Muss said suddenly.

Gozo nodded. 'Through the desert, if that's what you mean.'

Muss didn't say anything to that. Gozo glanced at him. Muss continued to watch the game.

Muss was about the same age as Gozo, but he was much smaller. He had fine, silky hair, and his eyes were bright, and he watched the game avidly. He loved playing WallBall, but he wasn't really good at it. Sometimes his tiny size was an advantage, and he was able to squeeze through a gap between an opponent and a wall, for example, where no one else could have gone. But in general, his hands were too small to grip the ball easily, and his arms were too small to reach in front of an opponent by surprise, and his legs were too small to carry him faster that the others, and . . . he was just too small to be a really good player. But he was a great thinker about the game, and understood all its possibilities and complexity better than any other boy of his age in Run.

There was no one who could have explained it better to a newcomer.

The game of WallBall, as it was played in Run, had one aim: to score more goals than the opposing team by getting the ball into the stone horns that stood in each corner of the court. Each team attacked towards two of the horns. But if this was the aim, the contest was governed by one great principle: you were not permitted to make contact with an opponent. This was the fundamental rule, and it was what gave the game its unique elegance, speed and dexterity. All of the individual rules—and there were many of them, often requiring difficult judgements by the umpires who adjudicated the tournaments—were designed to minimise the advantage that would be gained in a collision between two players. In short, in each situation, the rules penalised the player who had most to gain from a collision, and thus encouraged him to take steps to avoid it.

If two players came into contact, for example, the one with the ball would lose it if he was moving forward at the time. This prevented attackers trying to get past defenders by knocking them over, and made them find ways of sidestepping and evading defenders who threw themselves in their path. Therefore, according to a second rule, if the attacker was moving backward at the time of contact, avoiding the defender, *he* would get the penalty. And if he got past the defender? A player moving forward would get the free throw if he was closer to the goal than his opponent, thus discouraging defenders from knocking down attackers who had raced past them.

These were only some of the rules. What if two players were judged to be exactly side by side when they hit? What if they were both going for the ball? What if neither was going for the ball? There were rules to answer these questions, and rules to answer other questions, and sub-rules and exceptions. Over the years, a comprehensive set of laws had developed. Yet it was still possible, according to Muss, that something would happen that had never been thought of before, and an umpire might have to invent yet another rule on the spot. Gozo shook his head in amazement. Who could remember all these details? But that was the whole point, said Muss. That was the beauty of the game! It didn't matter if you couldn't remember the rules, they were for the umpires. As a player, all you had to do was to remember the principle. If you thought you could get an advantage by making contact, you were wrong. Whatever the relevant rule was, it would penalise you. The principle was simple. Remember it, stick to it, and the laws were on your side.

A skilful game of WallBall, played by two full teams of six a side, moved at incredible speed, the players throwing the ball or bouncing it off the walls with pin-point accuracy, catching with one hand, artfully evading one another, criss-crossing the court in complex patterns to create space and opportunity, and . . . all of it without contact, as if an invisible layer of air separated each player from his opponent.

By now, Muss seemed to have forgotten that it was Gozo's fault that he wasn't actually out on the court playing. Once he started talking about WallBall, nothing could stop him.

'Some players do try to draw the penalty. They think they're clever, but they're not. The rules are too smart. If your opponent's skilful, he'll twist around you at the last second and place himself in a position so *he* gets the penalty instead. And so he should! You deserve to lose the ball if you try to create a collision. The best players don't play for penalties. They just play for the ball and—' Muss stopped. '*Look*! Gandel's good at this. Watch what he does. He practises it all the time.'

Gandel had the ball a short distance from one of the horns. One opponent stood in front of him, and another stood guarding the goal itself. The other player on the opposite team, Bertram, stood halfway between Gandel and the horn in the other corner, to block a long throw in that direction. Gandel's two teammates, Hardy and Philp, circled nearby, waiting for a pass.

'Now, you watch,' whispered Muss. 'Hardy's going to run wide, and then he's going to cut back in and draw Bertram away from the other horn. Hardy knows how it works. And then Gandel's going to lob. It's a long throw, but it doesn't matter. Even if he misses, he'll be the first to get to the ball as long as Hardy takes Bertram away.'

Even before Muss had finished talking, Hardy had begun to swing out wide, and then he cut back inside Bertram, who moved forward to cover him. But Hardy kept running and moved back towards Gandel and before he realised what was happening Bertram was being drawn closer to Gandel as well and now Gandel rocked back and lobbed the ball over Bertram's head towards the far goal. And as soon as he released the ball, even before he saw whether it had gone in, he was charging after it, quick, tall and strong. The ball bobbled on the edge of the horn and fell out. But Bertram couldn't double back quickly enough, and by now Gandel was ahead of him, and a second later he gathered up the ball and slammed it into the horn. He went racing away down the court, pointing a finger and grinning up at Muss. Muss stood up and raised his arms in delight.

'I thought of that one! That's my move,' Muss said to Gozo when he sat down again, still beaming. '*I* could never do it. You have to be tall and fast, like Gandel.'

Gandel was back in the middle of the court now, breathing heavily. The others were walking back towards the centre.

'It's the Crow Festival in a month,' said Muss. 'Everyone gets to compete, us as well. We get to play against the older teams. But we can win. The boys' team has won in the past, I've heard people say it. Pfister said he'd help to train us, even though he'll be competing as well, but he hardly ever turns up. Doesn't matter, I've thought of all kinds of moves. WallBall isn't about strength, Gozo. It's speed and agility that count, and brains.'

'Is he ready to try now?' shouted Gandel from the centre of the court.

Muss looked inquiringly at Gozo. 'Want to try?'

Gozo grinned. 'Why not?' he said.

Muss nodded enthusiastically. They went down the stairs.

'Don't worry if you make a few mistakes,' said Muss. 'It's a complicated game. It takes years to learn it properly. If you give away a few penalties, it doesn't matter.'

Gozo was glad it didn't matter, because he gave away penalties galore. Everyone seemed to know how to trick him into touching them when the rules were in their favour. So much for not playing for penalties! Muss was the worst of the lot. He danced around and grinned happily each time he extracted a free throw from him. Gozo didn't know any of the moves which would have turned the advantage to him, and he soon realised that the other team was continuously using him to create opportunities. He fell for every trick. But he did still manage to get the ball a couple of times, and once he even swung and slapped the ball up the court, using the wall to bounce it back, and the truth was he didn't even look where he was throwing and hardly knew what he was doing but somehow Hardy was there on the other end of the pass and a second later he slammed the ball into the horn. And Gandel turned around and said: 'Pfister was right, he really *does* throw a good forward angle.'

And Gozo beamed with pleasure, and he thought, this game isn't so hard after all!

And then he looked up, as he walked back to the centre, and saw that someone was sitting on the grass, watching the game. It was the girl, the same girl he had seen with the flute, who was the most beautiful girl in the world.

He was glad she had seen that pass, because she must also have seen a lot of mistakes, and now that she was here, he couldn't stop thinking about her, and the more he thought about her, the more mistakes he made. He didn't know how to play this game and he wished she'd go away and at the same time he wished she wouldn't. He couldn't help glancing up at her, and every time he glanced up at her, he looked away at once, and every time he looked away, he couldn't help glancing back at her again.

Then they were finished, and Muss said: 'That was good, Gozo.' And even Gandel said it was good for someone who had just arrived from the desert. But all Gozo could think about was the girl, who was still watching from the other side of the court, and about everything she had seen, despite his one great forward angle to Hardy, all the mistakes and penalties he had given away, and he could hardly bear to imagine what she must think of him.

15

The days passed in Run like sunlight moving over the stones where the giant green lizards came out to bask, like the winds that blew across the cloudless sky and held the eagles high in the air: easy, steady, warm and pleasant.

Gozo and Muss became firm friends, and every day they went to the WallBall court where Gandel and the other boys gathered to play. When Muss assured them that Gozo really *was* from the desert, everyone wanted to find out more about him. His skill at the game increased as well, and soon he became known not only for his forward angle throw, but also for his ability to intercept a ball by a surprise leap from behind an opponent. The first time he did it, everyone thought it was a fluke. But then he found that he could do it again and again. This ability surprised him as much as anyone else. It made him a useful player, especially when his team was defending.

'Maybe you'll get to play at the Crow Festival,' said Muss.

'Do you think so?' said Gozo excitedly.

'Maybe,' said Muss. 'You have to give away fewer penalties, of course. I should teach you about that.'

And Muss taught him. He didn't have to. Only six of the boys could play on the team at the Crow Festival, with one reserve. That meant one of them was going to miss out, if Gozo played, and that one was probably going to be Muss. But Muss couldn't help himself, he taught Gozo everything he could. He loved the game so much, he wanted everyone to understand it as well as he did. Besides, he was the team's strategist, and even if he didn't actually play, they'd never be able to win without him.

'There's just one other thing,' said Muss, and he grinned mischievously. 'You always play badly when Anya's watching. You like her too much. You've got to ignore her, you get too nervous.'

Gozo went red. 'I do not like her. I've never even spoken to her.'

'Exactly!' said Muss in a knowing tone.

Ignore her, thought Gozo. Easy for Muss to say! Gozo didn't know what it was about Anya, or how it had happened, but whenever she came to the WallBall court to watch them practise, he could hardly think of anything but her. He thought about her at other times as well. Why? Why did he suddenly find himself thinking about someone else all the time, especially someone like Anya, who was so beautiful, and could play the flute, and probably thought *he* was just a clumsy WallBall player who gave away too many penalties and threw too many bad passes?

Not that he played WallBall *all* the time. Other teams practised as well, and he and Muss and the others sometimes watched them for a while, discussing the strategies they saw. Or he went with Muss to help look after the pigs, which were kept in a large ruined building not far from the turkeys. The pigs had come from a single pair which had been saved from a shipwreck many years before, and had been brought through the forest by one of the survivors. Muss went there every afternoon to help feed them. And there were other things to do in Run, either with Muss or the others. One day everyone turned out to harvest the corn from a field that had ripened, and after it was picked, they all carried it back to the HoneyCone, where the rooms on the lowest level served as an enormous storehouse. Afterwards, there was a big meal for everyone in front of the building. Bartlett and Jacques helped that day as well, and they took Gozo to meet Grandma Myrtle, whom he hadn't met before.

Of course, for someone who had just come from the outside, there were some strange things about the way people lived in Run. For a start, you could just take whatever you wanted. And when the fields had to be ploughed, sown or harvested, everyone helped. Yet the forest was so fruitful, the soil so rich, the land so abundant, that it required little labour to produce more than enough for everyone, and for every hour that people worked, they had two or three hours to sit, or walk, or talk, or eat, or play WallBall, or do whatever they chose. When you wanted cakes or corn bread, you went to the bakers, when you wanted turkey, you went to the roasters. If you needed cloth, you went to the spinners. Somehow there seemed to be a person to do each job that needed to be done, because each job attracted a person who wanted to do it.

Not that Bartlett and Jacques, or even Gozo, had to go off to get things for themselves very often. Every day Pfister arrived at the Circle House carrying a great basket of food, as if it were a task that someone had given him. He loved to sit and talk, and ask about the adventures Bartlett and Jacques had experienced, and hear about all the kinds of places that existed in the world. He always had a hundred things to do, of course, and was always slapping his forehead as he remembered something he had forgotten, but you soon learned to expect that from Pfister. He always seemed to have time to take Bartlett wherever he wanted. He took him to the part of the forest where the grove of quince trees grew, and together they climbed the trees and tossed down ripe yellow quinces, as big as your fist, and carried them to the bakers in bags slung over their shoulders. He took him to meet Boas, the carpenter, and the two pairs of twins who were Run's woodcutters. Together, they carried cotton to the cotton spinners, who spent every morning working in a long building where the air was thick with wisps of cotton, and spent each afternoon asleep under a pine tree outside. The twins had wanted to cut the pine tree down five years before, but the spinners wouldn't let them.

The twins knew every tree in Run as if it were their own creation, how quickly it would grow, how tall it would become, when it would be ready for felling. The forest around the buildings was their workroom, and they managed it carefully. They thinned it in places where it became too thick, making sure that the remaining trees had space to grow tall and strong. When the carpenter needed wood, they were the ones who provided it. They had a great understanding of trees and knew their nature just as a goldsmith knows the nature of gold and how best to fashion it. In a way, they were explorers as well, even if only of the forest, and Bartlett walked all over Run with them, gazing up at the trunks soaring above him and listening to the twins as they described how a particular tree had developed, what its history had been, how much longer it should be left. When they decided to fell one, Bartlett raised an axe and hewed into it with them, and even here there was much for him to learn, which side to cut, which direction it would fall, how to bring it down with least destruction to the surrounding trees.

If he had been born in Run, Bartlett began to think, this is the work he would have chosen. To be a woodcutter and a tree-feller, to know the nature of the forest as a goldsmith knows his metal . . . there was something good about this. Something wholesome and satisfying. A person could do this, Bartlett thought, and be happy.

And Jacques le Grand? Sometimes he went with Bartlett, and sometimes he didn't. Sometimes Gozo babbled so excitedly about WallBall that Jacques went to watch the game. And sometimes he went alone, out into Run, to walk its tracks, like a *true* explorer.

'Are you coming tomorrow?' said Bartlett one evening. 'Pfister says there's a pond, and apparently there's a certain plant that has a wonderful fruit. It grows just under the water, and you have to swim to harvest it.'

'Are there alligators?' said Gozo.

Bartlett grinned. 'I don't think so.'

'I'll come, then.'

'Jacques, what about you?'

Jacques shook his head.

'Why not?' said Bartlett. 'Listen, Jacques, why not enjoy yourself? How long have we spent in deserts and mountains over the years? When we find somewhere a bit more pleasant, why shouldn't we take the opportunity? You don't know when you'll have the chance again. Remember what Elwood Tucker said? It's the Forest of Plenty.'

But where was Elwood Tucker? What had happened to him? They had seen him once, spoken to him for a few minutes, and then he had vanished. Tucker helped the Falla, everyone said. What did that mean? What did he do? Where was he? How did he spend his days? And why hadn't they seen him again, as if one short conversation, after ten years, was enough?

That was what Jacques wanted to know. He was more interested in that than in any fruit, even one that grew under the water. And as for the Falla himself, Jacques wondered, why was it that they still hadn't been called to meet him?

Bartlett grinned.

'Always worrying, eh, Jacques?'

16

Jacques was walking alone. He wasn't far from the building where they had seen the Falla on their first day in Run. He recognised the place. By now, he recognised many places in Run, because he had been walking its tracks day after day, and when an explorer walks in a new place, and explores its tracks, he begins to put together a map of that place in his head, even if he doesn't realise he is doing it. But Jacques did realise he was doing it, and by now he could have sat down and drawn a map of the places he had explored in Run, just as he had once drawn a map of the entire Margoulis Caverns, if only he'd had paper and pencil with which to do it.

He turned away from the Falla's house. He had passed it often enough. Instead, Jacques followed a narrow path that he had seen but ignored before. The path led straight into a dense thicket of trees, and soon they were so close around him that their branches brushed at his shoulders and sometimes he had to duck to pass under them. Here, for some reason, the woodcutters had not been at work. It was like being back in the untouched forest. The path was barely more than a hint of a track. Jacques followed it further. Suddenly the path ended at a clearing and he saw a house. It was flat and long, with windows that were filled with a kind of carved stone grille. The house was in good condition. Its roof was still in place. The grille in the windows was especially striking, delicately worked, like squares of lace set into the walls. In the clearing, however, there were scattered lengths of white rock lying in the grass, as if there must once have been another building here, and it had fallen to pieces. Or maybe people had taken it apart, and these were the only fragments that were left.

It was strange, to see such a beautiful building, in such good condition, and yet the path to it was little more than wild forest.

The clearing was sunny. Jacques sat down on one of the pieces of rock.

Jacques turned his face up to the sun and closed his eyes. He felt just like a lizard, warming its blood with the sunlight. Suddenly he felt very drowsy. He opened his eyes again. The trees at the edge of the clearing merged in a liquid green blur. He felt light-headed. He didn't know what was happening to him. Maybe he was ill. He bowed his head, and closed his eyes again, and took a deep breath, hoping that when he looked up again he would feel better. And when he did look up again, there was Elwood Tucker, watching him.

Where had he come from? From the house? From the forest? Jacques still felt lightheaded. He felt as if he were swaying, as if he might topple backwards off the stone. A sweat had broken out on his forehead. He felt both hot and cold at the same time.

He heard Elwood Tucker's voice.

'You don't look well, Jacques.'

Jacques looked up at him again. Tucker came a little closer.

'Are you all right?'

Jacques nodded.

Tucker sat down on a piece of stone nearby. He started talking again. Jacques tried to concentrate, to understand what he was saying. He didn't know if he caught everything that Tucker said.

'Do you like it here, Jacques? They say Bartlett has been all over the place with Pfister . . . Pfister's a good lad. A little forgetful, sometimes, and not perfectly reliable. Not like we were, Jacques. Can you remember, when we were young? . . . Old Sutton Pufrock and his sayings! Inventiveness, Desperation and Reliability, the three tools of an explorer.'

'Perseverance,' muttered Jacques.

'What was that?'

'Perseverance, not Reliability,' repeated Jacques with effort.

'Really?' Elwood Tucker looked genuinely surprised. He shook his head in disbelief. 'Was it really Perseverance? Imagine that, I'd forgotten! Well, we had to be reliable as well. I suppose you can't be reliable if you don't persevere, so it's all the same, isn't it?'

No, thought Jacques, it isn't all the same. But he was

124

feeling too ill to say anything. He was feeling too . . . strange for this conversation. Couldn't Tucker see that? What was he talking about? Why this? Why now?

'How is he, by the way, old Pufrock? Still alive?'

Jacques nodded.

'He'll never die,' muttered Tucker, as much to himself as to Jacques. 'That fall on the Piuong Glacier should have killed a man half his age. But up he jumped, fit as a fiddle, as soon as we went down to get him, and kept on climbing. What else was it that he used to say? I remember! "If you stop because you can't be bothered, you'll never finish anything again." Something like that, wasn't it?'

Jacques took a deep breath, trying to steady himself.

'It *was* something like that, I'm sure. Sutton Pufrock and his sayings! I hated him. I really did.' Tucker paused, and this time Jacques managed to look up at him, and his gaze was held by the intensity of Tucker's eyes. 'Did you know that? I really, *really* hated him. No, you didn't know, of course not. How could you? Don't look at me like that. *You'd* never hate a man, would you, Jacques? Not you, not Jacques le Grand.'

Jacques blinked, trying to clear the haze that seemed to have settled over his mind. How could you *hate* Sutton Pufrock? How could you hate anyone? Jacques had never truly, fully hated any other person in his life. He always found something to value, even if a person irritated or dismayed him from time to time. Even Elwood, whom he had never really liked, had his good points.

Yet Elwood hated Sutton Pufrock. You only had to

look at his face to tell. And was it really him, Elwood Tucker, after all this time? Nothing seemed real. Was he really alive, the promising young explorer with the flowing hair, and was this *him*, this bald man with hatred blazing in his eyes?

'You still haven't told me. Do you like it here, Jacques?' asked Elwood Tucker once more.

Jacques wiped the sweat from his forehead. He wanted to get out of this clearing. He wanted to get away from these stones lying in the grass.

But Tucker was still talking, questioning. His voice went on, prodding, probing, and every word seemed to drain another drop of Jacques' strength.

'Bartlett seems to be enjoying himself. He knows how to make the best of anything, Bartlett. And that boy you brought with you, he's made some friends. He's become a bit of a WallBaller, hasn't he? You see, I know all about it. But you, Jacques. What about you? What are *you* doing? You're the one to worry about, aren't you? I'm right. We both know I'm right. What about *you*, Jacques? What about you?'

What about him? Jacques tilted back and stared up at the sky, opening his mouth to catch a breath of air. The sweat was running off his face. Thoughts raced through his head, all out of order, all disconnected. The sky was so blue, it seemed to pour down on top of him, like a liquid, like water, all around him, submerging him, drowning him.

The voice was coming from far away. 'What about you, Jacques? What about you? What about you . . .'

126

Jacques opened his eyes. He blinked. All he could see was blueness. He was staring at the sky. Why? He turned his head and felt a sharp pain. He was lying on his back. He put his hand behind his neck and felt something wet. He looked at his fingers. There was blood on them. He felt again, and discovered the corner of a stone under his neck. He must have cut himself. He must have fallen backwards and cut himself. Why? He must have fainted. Yes, he *had* fainted, that was it. He could remember it now, the sweating, the weakness, then blacking out. And before that? Before that, he remembered, there was Elwood Tucker.

Jacques le Grand sat up. He took a deep breath. He looked around. The clearing was empty. Elwood Tucker was gone.

17

'What are we doing here, Bartlett?' said Jacques.

Bartlett looked at Jacques for a moment before answering. A puzzled smile came across his lips. 'Having breakfast?'

Jacques shook his head.

Gozo laughed. They definitely *were* having breakfast, and Pfister, who had brought the food, was having it with them. There were thick slices of corn bread in front of them, and a big pot of mango jam, and a plate of sweets made out of honey and nuts, called kifta, which was a breakfast specialty of Run. There was also a basket of the special, luscious fruit they had collected yesterday from the pond.

'Pfister,' said Jacques, 'would you mind leaving us?'

Pfister looked at Bartlett. Bartlett glanced at Jacques, then he nodded. 'You'd better go, Pfister. I'll see you later.'

'At the bakers'?'

Bartlett didn't reply. Pfister got up. He stood there for a moment longer, and then, reluctantly, walked to the path that led away through the forest.

Gozo waited to find out what Jacques was talking about. But Bartlett already knew.

'There's nothing wrong with resting here for a while, Jacques,' said Bartlett. 'Explorers are allowed to rest. You know what Sutton Pufrock used to say: "When you feel—"'

Jacques nodded abruptly. He knew what Sutton Pufrock used to say, he didn't need Bartlett to remind him.

'All right,' said Bartlett.

But it wasn't all right, and Bartlett could see it. Something really was worrying Jacques. And Bartlett had known him long enough to realise that if something was worrying Jacques, really worrying him, then he ought to be worried as well.

'Jacques, we'll just rest here until we're ready—'

'Three weeks. It's already been three weeks, Bartlett!'

'What's three weeks? We're not in a hurry, are we?'

'Time moves slowly in Run,' said Jacques quietly.

Bartlett stared. 'You've *seen* him, haven't you?'

Jacques nodded.

'Seen who?' said Gozo.

'He knows what's going on, Bartlett. Don't think he doesn't. He knows everything. He knows what you've been doing. He says you're enjoying yourself. He knows Gozo plays WallBall. And me, he said. What about me?

129

I'm the one, he said. What do you think he meant by that?'

'*Who?*' cried Gozo in frustration. 'Who are you talking about?'

Bartlett shook his head. This was turning into quite a speech for Jacques! It was always eerie to hear Jacques making a speech, and he never did it lightly. If Bartlett needed convincing to think about something seriously, a speech from Jacques was enough.

'What are you saying, Jacques?' he asked

'I'm saying it's time to leave.'

'Mr Bartlett!' exclaimed Gozo. 'We're not leaving yet, are we?'

Bartlett continued to stare at Jacques.

'I'm saying it's time to go, Bartlett. We're rested. We're more than rested. We're starting to *settle*.'

Gozo looked anxiously at Jacques, then back at Bartlett. 'Mr Bartlett,' he cried again, 'I don't what you're talking about, and I don't know who Jacques is meant to have seen, but . . . I'm not leaving! I'm not. It's only a week to the Crow Festival, and Gandel says I can play if I stop giving so many penalties. So I'm not leaving, just *see* if I am!'

And Gozo jumped up and ran out of the Circle House, not even pausing to take a handful of kifta with him.

Neither Bartlett nor Jacques moved to go after him.

'We're starting to settle?' whispered Bartlett.

Jacques nodded. 'You are, Bartlett. It's easy, isn't it? Tell me . . .' Jacques paused. It was hard for him to continue, to say what he had to say. He and Bartlett had travelled together so long, explored together so much, saved each other's lives so often, that it had hardly ever crossed Jacques' mind to imagine that all of this might end. He took a deep breath. 'Tell me, do you *want* to stay here?'

Bartlett looked at him abruptly.

'Just tell me,' said Jacques. 'If you want to stay, it's all right, but just tell me. That's all I ask. I can get out of this forest alone, you know it as well as I do. I can get out of it with the boy, as well, if you want me to take him back to his uncle.'

Bartlett didn't reply. He stared at Jacques, frowning, but his gaze went right through him, as if he were looking not at Jacques, but at a reflection of something new, dark and strange within himself.

'No, don't ask what I think,' said Jacques. 'It's up to you. But I won't be staying, Bartlett. What kind of a place is this? People are happy. They have plenty to eat, enough to wear. They play games, they do what they want to do. It's good, I suppose. But it isn't the first pleasant place we've seen. Do you remember the Valley of Hale? The Shadroch Plains?'

'They weren't as pleasant as this,' murmured Bartlett.

'No, but they were pleasant enough. Yet we didn't stay. Just to live, even to live happily, has never been enough for us. We've always wanted to find more, to discover more. We've never been content with what we know, but with what we can find out.' Jacques paused. He shrugged. 'But people change, Bartlett. You said it yourself. All I'm saying is . . . if you've changed, tell me. Tell *me*? Bartlett, if you've changed, it's time to admit it to yourself.'

Bartlett's gaze dropped. He stared long and hard at his worn, weathered boots. They had taken him across the world, up the slopes of mountains and deep into caves. But every pair of boots, eventually, must be laid aside.

Jacques waited.

Finally Bartlett looked up. Then he grinned. 'No one changes that much. That's what *you* said, isn't it?'

Jacques looked at him for a moment longer, then he grinned as well.

'It is pleasant, though, isn't it?' said Bartlett.

'Shall I tell you why it's so easy to settle here? Not only because it's so pleasant. That's only part of it, not the main reason. Bartlett, this is the thing: everyone's *expecting* us to stay. Haven't you noticed? Think about it. The things people say to us, the way they behave. This place isn't like anywhere else we've ever been. That's the difference between here and the Shadroch Plains. There, when strangers arrive, the first thing people ask is when they're going to leave. But not here.'

Bartlett did think about it. He nodded. Jacques was right!

'Bartlett, can't you see? As far as they're concerned, we're never going to go.'

Bartlett and Jacques strode swiftly along the path from the Circle House. Bartlett's mind was working rapidly. He felt as if someone had just slapped him on the face. Suddenly, he was *awake*. Everything that Jacques had said was right. And he was right to have said it. It's the responsibility of any explorer to tell another what he thinks, even if the other doesn't necessarily want to hear it. It's not only the responsibility of any explorer, it's the responsibility of any friend.

They came to the building where they had first seen the Falla. It loomed above them, the high wall, then the platform, then the structure on top of the platform. They walked around it. There were no stairs. There were three doors on one side of the lower level, all closed. Everything was still. The only noise came from the birds in the trees around them.

Bartlett glanced at Jacques, shrugged, and cupped his hands around his mouth.

'Falla!'

They stopped to listen. Bartlett called out again.

'*Falla!*'

There was no reply.

They waited, staring up at the blank walls in front of them. Bartlett felt foolish, shouting 'Falla'. They didn't even know whether he was inside. Besides, a Falla might not necessarily want someone shouting his name like that. Yet there was no other way. Bartlett called out a third time.

No answer.

'What now, Jacques? Maybe we should find Pfister.'

Jacques didn't look convinced.

'Who then?'

They thought for a moment. Then they both looked at each other, and they knew.

18

Grandma Myrtle was at her loom. She was working on the same Lou-Lou tapestry that she had been working on when the explorers first met her, showing the bird taking off from a branch. It wasn't unusual for Grandma Myrtle to work on a single piece for weeks, sometimes months, and it was nothing for her to unpick and redo a section two, three or even four times until it was perfect—or as close to perfect as she could make it. Only the living Lou-Lou itself was truly perfect, and even though Grandma Myrtle spent her whole life trying to reproduce that perfection, she doubted that it was possible.

She looked around when they arrived in her doorway, and turned back to finish the work she had started.

'I was wondering how long it would take,' she said, threading the strands with her long, elegant fingers. 'The very first time I saw you, I knew you'd be the ones. Wait a moment. If I stop in the middle, it'll ruin everything.'

'So, you were trying to find the Falla,' said Grandma Myrtle, after she finally let her arms fall from the loom and had swivelled herself around to face them.

'Yes,' said Bartlett. 'Where can we find him? We have something to tell him.'

'Let me guess. You're leaving?'

Bartlett nodded.

'Leaving . . .' Grandma Myrtle repeated the word as if it were an object, a cold, hard *thing*, like a piece of rock, without meaning.

She gestured at the table beside her, where there was a plate of cakes. Bartlett and Jacques shook their heads.

She sighed. 'At first, you know, my husband wanted to leave. He even made plans. He collected a month's supply of food. We didn't know what to take. Heaven knows how he thought we were going to carry it!'

'What happened?' said Bartlett.

'Oh, nothing. We never left. In the end, we never even tried. After a while, it was hard to see why we should. I mean, it's very unlikely we would have survived. And what else could we want, anyway? We lacked for nothing here. If we needed any persuading, George convinced us.'

'George?'

Grandma Myrtle chuckled. 'I don't know when he started calling himself the Falla. What a name! Where did he get it from? Someone who was already here said it was the ancient name of the ruler of Run, but how would he have known? He's my brother, you know.'

'The Falla's your *brother*?'

'Yes. George is. He was always a very determined man. If it wasn't for him, I don't think we would have survived after the shipwreck. He was travelling with my husband and me. We were poor, we were young, Bartlett, and we were off to seek a new life abroad. When we stopped at Gavingar, and took that carriage ride to the edge of the desert, we spent the last penny we had. We didn't care! We were going to a new land, and we'd find everything we needed there. That's what we thought. When the ship sank, only five of us survived. And I think we would have stayed right there on the beach, until we died, if George hadn't convinced us to set off into the forest. The other two didn't have the courage to come with us. They said a ship would come, a ship *must* come and save them.' Grandma Myrtle shook her head at the memory. 'I'm sure they perished. Oh, it wasn't easy for us, don't imagine it was. We starved in the forest, Bartlett, we were desperate. We went half mad in the darkness and the damp. And the noise, the noise! If I'd known what it would be like, I don't think I would have had the courage to start. I would have stayed on the beach as well. But finally, when we were literally *crawling*, we found this place. Another day and it would have been the end of us, I'm sure. How could we imagine going through that again? And why should we? What else could we want, once we were here? Who could ask for more?' Grandma Mrytle sighed. 'Elwood Tucker calls it the Forest of Plenty, doesn't he? He's right, that's what it is. But it's funny, when we were on our way here, when we were right in the middle of it, we almost died of hunger.'

Bartlett nodded. He waited. Grandma Myrtle knew she hadn't answered Bartlett's original question. She knew she hadn't told him what he had come to find out.

'George has changed, Bartlett. Look at him. What's happened to him? He's blown up. He eats, he gorges. Even the last time I saw him, he was huge. I can't imagine what he must be like now! Have you seen him?

Oh, I wish he'd never taken that title. The Falla! From the day he called himself that, he's never been the same. He knows no restraint. He's encouraged in his folly. And who is it that encourages him? Who?'

'Where is he? He must be somewhere.'

Grandma Myrtle shook her head. 'You won't find him. I never see him now. I haven't seen him for years. Can you believe that? He never comes out of his house. I don't think of him as my brother any more. I think of him as the *Falla*. The *Falla* stays in his house, and no one sees him unless Elwood Tucker wants them to.'

Now the woman stopped and looked at them closely, both Bartlett and Jacques. Now she had come to the point.

'But you know what Elwood Tucker's like, don't you? Didn't you say you knew him before he came here?'

'He's changed,' said Bartlett. 'He's not the same as—'

Bartlett stopped. Grandma Myrtle was laughing. She shook her head, and there was even the hint of a tear in her eye.

'Changed?' she said eventually, when she had stopped laughing and recovered her breath. 'Elwood Tucker? Changed, you say? Bartlett, I've known that man for ten years, and he hasn't changed since the day I first laid eyes on him.'

19

While Bartlett and Jacques were trying to find the Falla, Elwood Tucker was with him. The ex-explorer knew that time was running out. He had sensed it even before he found Jacques le Grand sitting in the clearing in front of his house, and now he felt it with certainty. It had been a surprise, to come across Jacques like that. The thickness of the forest around his house kept people out. Yet Jacques had found his way through it. How long would he and Bartlett be prepared to wait in Run? They had already been here three weeks, and for an explorer, three weeks was a considerable time. How much longer before they tried to leave?

Even the Falla knew it, or perhaps he only sensed Elwood's preoccupation.

'Don't you think I should see them?' he said, watching the other man from his couch.

Elwood Tucker looked at him as coolly as he could. 'Why?'

The Falla shrugged. 'Just to see how they're getting along. People don't always find it easy to settle in.'

Elwood hesitated. The Falla might have grown too fat to get off his couch, but behind those tiny eyes, half hidden in the folds of his face, there was still much shrewdness. Elwood knew it from experience.

'I've seen to everything,' said the ex-explorer cautiously.

'Where are they living?'

'The Circle House.'

'That's right. You told me,' said the Falla.

The girl, who was at her father's feet, as usual, stared at him.

'Pfister's been looking after them,' said Tucker. 'They've been recovering from their ordeal in the forest. The boy's started playing WallBall. He's getting quite good, apparently. And Bartlett spends his time with the twins. Maybe he'll end up as one of our woodcutters. After all, it's a bit like exploration. You have to know the place like the back of your hand.'

The Falla didn't look convinced. 'I thought you said Bartlett's like you, Elwood. If he's anything like you, he won't be satisfied cutting wood. He'll want to do something more interesting. He'll want to *think* a bit.'

Elwood Tucker smiled contemptuously. 'We were both explorers, Falla, but that's as far as the similarity goes. Between you and me, Bartlett wasn't exactly the brightest log in the woodpile. The best explorers often aren't, you know.'

'But I thought you said *you* were the best explorer before you came to Run.'

Elwood Tucker couldn't tell if the Falla was serious or mocking. '*Often*,' he said evenly. 'I said explorers aren't *often* the brightest. There are exceptions.'

The Falla grinned. The heavy folds of his face creased, and his eyes disappeared entirely. Out of the corner of his eye, Elwood saw the girl grinning at him as well.

'Come on, Elwood! Where's your sense of humour? You let yourself in for that one.'

Tucker smiled grudgingly. The Falla was a tactless man, he had often thought, and someone ought to teach him a little discretion.

'You know I'm only teasing,' said the Falla. He reached out for a handful of sweets, and before he ate them, he said: 'Where would I be without you?'

Exactly, thought Elwood Tucker, as he watched the Falla eat. Where *would* you be?

After a moment the Falla looked at the ex-explorer again. 'Wasn't there a third one? You haven't mentioned him.'

'Jacques le Grand.'

'That's the one. Well?' said the Falla.

Elwood Tucker shrugged. 'He's all right.'

'What does that mean, "He's all right"?'

'It means he won't cause any trouble. I know him.'

The Falla didn't look satisfied. Maybe he suspected something from the way Tucker said it, or from the expression on his face. 'What's he doing with himself?' he asked.

Elwood shrugged. 'He walks around, looks at things. He's an explorer, Falla. That's what explorers do.'

The Falla gripped the edge of the couch with his fingers and began to haul himself upright. It was a lengthy operation. Eventually he was sitting up, puffing, with his legs over the edge of the couch.

He took some time to recover from the exercise. Then he looked up and poked a finger in Elwood's direction.

'*You* could have left,' he said.

Tucker didn't even blink. He stared stonily at the

Falla, as if he had no idea what he was talking about.

'You *could* have left,' repeated the Falla.

Tucker glanced at the girl. Her eyes were on him. He wished the Falla would send her away. He didn't want to talk about this in front of her. The Falla should have known better. It wasn't safe. It wasn't prudent.

But when it came to his daughter, the Falla wasn't prudent at all.

'What was that story you told me when they arrived, Elwood? I've been thinking about it. I've been trying to remember the day *you* arrived. You weren't starving, you weren't frightened. You weren't a skeleton. You knew exactly what you were doing. No one else ever came out of the forest like that—not until your friends appeared, anyway. They were exactly like you were. Strong, healthy, fit. Skeletons! If they were skeletons, then so am I!'

The Falla wasn't a skeleton. He was as far from being a skeleton as a man can be.

'Eh, Anya?' said the Falla. 'They weren't skeletons, were they?'

Anya shook her head.

'Recovering from their ordeal! What were those things you told me, Elwood? Digging for roots with their fingernails? Did they really have no food left? Is that the truth?'

Elwood Tucker said nothing.

The Falla's voice dropped. 'What were *you* doing, Elwood? You've always told me you got lost, but I never really believed you.' The Falla paused. 'I know what you were really doing. You were crossing the forest, weren't you? You were crossing it from side to side, and that's how you found us.'

For one last moment, Elwood Tucker hesitated. His mind raced, trying to find a way out. But there wasn't one. When he spoke, his voice was cold.

'You always said I could never fool you, Falla.'

The Falla waited.

Tucker smiled grimly. 'You're right. I was crossing the forest, from side to side, methodically, if you must know. Criss-crossing it, so when I went back I would be able to say I'd covered it all, and that all the stories and myths were false. *I* was going to prove it.'

'I knew it! I knew it even then. You said you were lost,

143

but I knew it was a lie.' The Falla shook his head at his own willingness to be deceived. 'I've known it for ten years.'

'Yet you convinced yourself it was true,' said Elwood. The girl watched, but now he had forgotten about her. 'I could have walked out of here, like *that*.' He clicked his fingers. 'Do you have any idea what it takes to be able to do that? Do you have any idea of the abilities it requires, to do it, alone?'

'But you didn't,' murmured the Falla. 'Why not? Why did you stay?'

'Why did you take the risk that I would leave?'

The Falla laughed. 'And do what? How could I have stopped you? Locked you up? For how long? Killed you?'

Tucker's lip curled contemptuously. 'You know what *I* would have done? I would have—'

He stopped. It was then, at that moment, that Bartlett's voice was heard. It came in through the three oval openings in the roof.

'*Falla!*'

The Falla's eyes went wide. 'What's that?' he whispered.

Elwood put a finger to his lips.

'*Falla!*'

Elwood glanced at the girl. If she made a move, uttered a sound, he decided, he would grab her. He didn't care what the Falla would say.

There was a longer pause. Then again: '*Falla!*'

The Falla looked nervously around the room. His eyes darted from side to side. Elwood watched him. The Falla was scared. Now, the ex-explorer knew, was the time to speak, now was the time to be the Falla's friend again, to be his eyes and ears.

'Falla . . .' he whispered.

The Falla jumped. 'What?'

'Falla, you know what will happen if they leave. Word will get out. They'll draw a map. Do you think we're so well hidden? In reality, we aren't far from the coast. An expedition from a ship, with a map, properly equipped, could reach us in a fortnight. And what will happen then? You know it yourself, Falla. First, the adventurers will arrive, looking for gold in the old buildings. They'll tear everything down, stone by stone, everything we have. And after they've destroyed everything, others will follow, attracted by the richness of the soil. But they won't understand where this richness comes from, not like we do, Falla. They won't know how you have to care for it, how you have to change the fields and let the forest replenish itself. They're not like us, Falla. They'll be impatient, greedy. They'll cut the forest down, and work the soil too hard and make it poor and barren, and eventually they'll leave as well, and nothing will be left but desert. Run will be desert, Falla, more desert to add to all the other desert the world already has.'

'I know,' whispered the Falla. 'I know. That's why you stayed, isn't it? That's why you never left.'

'What will you do if I bring them to you? Will you tell them they're free to go? Is that what you'll say?'

The Falla shook his head nervously. 'No . . . I don't know . . .'

'What *will* you say?'

The Falla frowned. He didn't reply.

'Then leave them to me,' said Elwood Tucker. He narrowed his eyes. 'They're in the Circle House, remember?'

Tucker waited. The Falla must know what he meant. He knew the secret of the Circle House. This was his chance to object. If he said nothing now, what was it but a sign of agreement?

The Falla hesitated. Suddenly he turned his face away, as if he couldn't bear to meet the ex-explorer's eyes. It was so long since he had left his house, so long since he had decided anything without Elwood Tucker's advice and recommendation, that now, even if he wanted to, he barely knew how to oppose him.

Elwood Tucker came out of the Falla's house. He leaned against the wall and pondered.

No, it wasn't so straightforward. That was the problem. He had told the Falla to leave the explorers to him, but what exactly he should do with them, he still didn't know.

He gazed at the top of the HoneyCone, rising above the trees in the distance. Then he turned and looked along a path and saw ears of corn waving in the sunlight. He could remember when they had cleared and planted that field, only two years before. Yet now, when he looked at the HoneyCone, at the field, he saw it all as he had seen it when he first arrived at Run ten years before, as a new, strange place . . . totally unexpected.

And he had decided to stay.

Why? He had never told anybody, had barely admitted it to himself.

It was so easy, wasn't it? So easy to go to bed each night and wake up the next morning in a place where everything was plentiful, amongst people who demanded nothing from you. So easy just to stay, and never go back into that dark torment of the forest floor, and hack your way through the branches, and be all alone with the birds screeching above your head until you found your way back out to the world again. So easy to 'settle', as explorers would say.

No, that wasn't it. That wasn't the *whole* of it. Be honest, Elwood. Getting through the forest again wasn't the problem, it was what would happen once you came out the other side. How much longer could you have kept going? Every exploit more dangerous, more difficult than the one before. Always having to prove you were the best. Faster, higher, steeper, colder, darker, further . . . Your nerves were starting to crack. In a way, you *were* going crazy in that forest. Not from hunger, or from fear, but from what was going to come next. What would you do after you had finished with the forest? And what would you do after that? And after that? How was it going to end? Never. How could it end? There was no way out. You'd have to keep going and going and going until you killed yourself proving that you were the best . . . that you were better than Bartlett.

And all along, you knew you weren't. You were a bit more cunning, perhaps, than Bartlett, and a bit more agile, perhaps, than Jacques, but they were the ones with real strength. It wasn't the Inventiveness, or the Desperation, it was the Reliability . . . no, the Perseverance, they were the ones with the real *Perseverance*, they would keep going, you knew, long after you had given up. You could run faster, but they would run longer. You could feel them, remember? You could *feel* them almost as if they were beasts breathing down your neck, even while you were all alone in that terrible forest. *They* would keep going and going and going. Sutton Pufrock was right. Perseverance, that was what you needed. And you never had it, or not enough of it, because having *enough* of it meant having more of it than Bartlett and Jacques. Nothing less would do.

So why not stop? Just stop, here, where no one would ever find you . . . and give up?

That was the truth. That was what he had done.

Elwood Tucker stared at the top of the HoneyCone. His gaze fixed itself on the single doorway just below the top.

He shook his head, smiling helplessly. He could remember the exact moment he decided to do it. He had been lying in the Circle House, where the Falla had put him, with his head on a pillow, staring at the roof, and suddenly he had thought: There *is* a way out. This is it, here. Do it! Just stay here, and no one will ever know.

And at that moment, he could remember, it was as if he felt an enormous weight being lifted off him.

But he didn't realise, at that moment, that another weight would soon replace it. It was all right for an explorer to give up—everyone did eventually—and maybe it was all right for him as well, even though he was still young. But it wasn't all right to give up like this. Other explorers would assume he had perished. They'd talk abut him sadly, honour his memory. Old Sutton Pufrock, his teacher, would even shed a tear, because he had become emotional with age, and regarded all his explorers as his own children. And he, Elwood Tucker, would have no right to this, none at all, because all along he would be living safely in Run!

And this weight, this guilt, never went away.

At first he hoped it would, but eventually he knew that he would never be free of it. Then there was a period when he had thought about leaving once more, going out through the forest, but he imagined what people would say when he suddenly reappeared, three, four, five years after he had gone, the questions they would ask and the things he would have to admit, and he pushed the thought of leaving aside. No, he decided, there was no going back. But this didn't drive the guilt away. On the very night he made this decision . . . he had the nightmare for the first time.

Ever since that night, it was always the same nightmare, with only slight variations. Sometimes he dreamt it three nights in a row, and sometimes he didn't dream it for a month. In the nightmare, he would be standing in front of the HoneyCone and suddenly someone would come out of the forest. At once, he would know that the person had come to get him. So he would start running, and the person would run after him. Sometimes he ran down one path, and sometimes down another. In some of the dreams he just ran around and around the Honey-Cone. But always the pursuer was just behind him, no matter how fast he ran, until suddenly, he would look behind him and the person had disappeared. Then he would have a terrible feeling of dread, because he knew that when he looked ahead again . . . the pursuer would be there, right in front of him! Then the person caught him and dragged him into the trees, into the darkness, away from Run, and—here the nightmare always stopped, and he would awake in a cold sweat, as if it were too awful even to dream about what would happen when he faced the world and everyone learned what he had done. And in the worst version of this nightmare, the one from which he awoke with the greatest sense of dread, the person who caught him was Bartlett, and Jacques le Grand was with him.

Was it just a nightmare? Sometimes he thought it wasn't. Who draws the line between dream and prophecy? Who else but Bartlett and Jacques had the ability to cross the forest? Sometimes he felt that he was merely waiting for it to happen. As time passed, perhaps, he actually began to expect it. So that day, when the girl came in and said that strangers had arrived at the HoneyCone, he didn't even need to hear her repeat their names. It was very strange. He *knew* who was out there. Even as he waited for the Falla to walk out onto the plat-form, he had been calm. He almost felt a sense of relief. It was as if he had been preparing for this moment for years, and now it was actually happening, now he could finally stop dreaming about it and face them in the flesh.

And when he walked out onto the platform, and looked down at the clearing . . . it was them. The ten years simply fell away. It was them, a little older, of course, and accompanied by some spiky-haired whipper-snapper, but *them*, Bartlett and Jacques le Grand, as if they had stepped living and breathing straight out of his nightmare and onto the grass beneath the Falla's house.

So they had come, and he had faced them, but after all it wasn't like the dream. They didn't drag him off. And now, what was he going to do with them?

They wouldn't stay, he knew they wouldn't. They were growing restless. Why else had they just been calling out for the Falla? Suddenly, as Elwood thought about them, all the old resentment came flooding back. They still felt they were better than him! They had probably even guessed why he had stayed in Run. Jacques was the one, deep, quiet, too thoughtful, always had been. They were laughing at him. Soon they would be telling everyone in Run what they knew, soon everyone else would be laughing at him as well. And the Falla? They would tell him, and he would be laughing as well. Elwood Tucker, the *great* Elwood Tucker, the intrepid explorer who had just given up because he couldn't—

Elwood Tucker gave a start. He had heard something. He turned. The girl was watching him from the edge of the clearing. She had come out of the building, the sly creature, with barely a sound. As soon as he spotted her, she skipped off into the trees.

He shook his head. If only he could clear his mind.

What if they left? No. They would tell what they had found. People would come. What he had said to the Falla was true. Everything would be destroyed. People are never content for others to be happy without trying to seize that happiness for themselves. The secret of Run was its secrecy.

And *him*? His secret was his secrecy as well. If they were allowed to leave, the whole world would know. Sutton Pufrock would know.

But if they stayed? For him, that was no better. Maybe it was worse. He would be a laughing-stock. The Falla would ridicule him. His influence would be destroyed. And how could he make them stay, anyway? It wasn't in their nature.

But if they left? No, no, he had already thought about that. So what to do? What to do with them?

The ex-explorer began to pace around the Falla's house, frowning, grimacing. There was no answer. He couldn't let them leave, he didn't want them to stay. But he had to do something. He had to act. If not, they'd take the decision out of his hands. They might even leave today! They were capable of it, those two, they could easily just walk away, even without provisions. They were capable of living off the forest. The ex-explorer knew what they were capable of, because he had once been capable of it himself.

What to do? What to do? He paced restlessly. He needed time. If he had time, he told himself, he could think about it clearly. He wouldn't feel so rushed. That's what he needed, more time. Put them where they couldn't get away. If he could just be *sure* they weren't about to leave, he could think about it clearly. He could make up his mind.

Put them where they couldn't get away . . . Yes. Elwood Tucker smiled grimly. Well, that part was easy. All along, he had known he might have to do it. Wasn't that why he had chosen the Circle House for them in the first place?

Where were they now? Looking for the Falla. But they wouldn't find him. And then? Back to the Circle House. Back they would come. Back they would come, and find him waiting for them. Elwood Tucker almost laughed out loud. It would be as easy as trapping a pair of raccoons.

20

The ball slapped against the wall and went skidding across the grass. Gozo got to it ahead of Bertram. Muss was further up the court, calling out and wriggling like an eel behind Hardy. Gozo threw the ball hard. It was a wild pass, went over Muss' head, bounced off the wall and straight into Gandel's hand. Gandel pelted the ball back along the side wall. Bertram raced after it. He changed direction, swerving right and cutting across Gozo's path. Gozo clipped his heel and sent him sprawling. Penalty. Bertram tossed the ball confidently into the horn.

'Nice pass, Gozo,' called out Gandel, as they regrouped in the centre, 'thanks a lot.'

'What's wrong?' whispered Muss. 'You're playing terribly. What kind of a throw was that? And how could you give away that penalty? You haven't given a penalty like that in a long time. It's the oldest trick of the lot. I've told you, Gozo, when they cut in front of you, you swing back and turn—'

'I know, ' muttered Gozo.

'Then why didn't you do it?'

Gozo shook his head. He couldn't concentrate. Walking out on Bartlett and Jacques . . . he had never done anything like that before. But were they really going to leave? He felt so upset, he just wanted to throw the ball as hard as he could every time he got it. And he didn't care about penalties. He'd felt like really *kicking* Bertram instead of just getting tangled up with his heel.

Muss nudged his arm. 'Look who's here,' he said.

Gozo looked up. Anya was watching. Gozo's heart sank. That was all he needed!

He glanced at Muss. Muss was grinning.

'I'm going,' said Gozo suddenly.

'Gozo,' said Gandel, 'we're playing fours!'

'Well, play threes,' he said, and he turned his back on Anya and walked off to the stairs.

Muss ran after him. 'Come on, Gozo, everyone has bad games. Look at me! I hardly ever have a *good* game.'

Gozo shook his head. He kept going. By now he had climbed out of the WallBall court and was walking towards the forest.

'I told you not to worry about Anya,' said Muss, still hurrying alongside him. 'You've got to forget about her.'

'It's not her.'

'It is. Everyone can see it.'

'It's not her. It's got nothing to do with her.'

'She likes you,' said Muss.

Gozo stopped. He looked closely at Muss. 'She does not!'

'And you like her.'

Gozo blushed a fiery red. He punched Muss in the shoulder.

Muss laughed. 'You do. You like her.

155

Do you want me to introduce you?'

'Muss!' growled Gozo.

Muss laughed again. 'Doesn't matter, anyway. She's so odd, I bet she'd run away if you tried to talk to her. She's a strange girl, Anya. Everyone says so.'

Did Gozo care what *everyone* said? He couldn't remember asking.

'The way she plays that flute . . .'

'I like the way she plays that flute,' murmured Gozo, without thinking first.

'I know you do!' said Muss.

Gozo punched him in the shoulder again. Muss grinned.

But Gozo wasn't in the mood to joke. 'I'm going,' said Gozo, 'I've got things to do.'

'What have you got to do?' called Muss, as Gozo began to walk away.

'Things,' shouted Gozo, without looking back.

Gozo walked. He did have to do something, he could feel it, but he didn't know what. He didn't know where he was going. He kept walking. He went to the bakers and got a cake and took a bite, but he didn't even feel like eating and he threw half of it away. Everything was disturbed and disordered inside him and he would have liked to ask Mr Bartlett about it but Mr Bartlett, this time, was part of the problem and so it wasn't necessarily the easiest thing to ask him what to do about it. But he would have to go back, he knew it, sooner or later. He couldn't put it off forever, he had to go back to the Circle House.

Crossing the clearing, Gozo could hear voices. He stopped outside the house, listening by the door.

'We're leaving. This is a wonderful place, and everyone has welcomed us, but it's time for us to go.'

That was Bartlett. Gozo clenched his fists angrily. Why didn't they ask *him* what he wanted?

Another voice answered. But it wasn't Jacques le Grand. It wasn't Pfister. Gozo frowned. Where had he heard that voice before?

'I knew you'd want to leave. I just wanted to be sure. I wanted to hear it from your lips.'

Gozo slipped quietly around the corner of the Circle House, where he wouldn't be seen if someone came out. He stared at the ground, listening hard. He heard the unfamiliar voice again .

'I know what you're thinking. You wouldn't stay, would you? Not *you*.'

Bartlett's voice replied: 'It doesn't matter to us why you chose to stay. I can see why you might want to. That was your decision. We're not judging you.'

'Aren't you?'

'No. Right, Jacques?'

'Do you think I care if you judge me or not? Do you think you're even in a *position* to judge me?'

'I don't know what you mean,' said Bartlett.

The other voice didn't answer. For a moment there was silence. Then there was a harsh clanking sound, shouts of surprise. Gozo didn't know what to do! What was happening? Did Bartlett and Jacques need his help? Should he run inside?

'Be quiet!' said the unfamiliar voice. 'Nothing will happen to you. Just be quiet.'

Gozo listened. After a moment he heard Bartlett's voice again.

'What do you want?'

'Time,' said the other voice.

A man came out. Gozo hugged the wall. The man crossed the clearing without turning to see Gozo hiding around the corner.

But Gozo knew who it was. The lean, bald-headed figure strode quickly to the path, and was gone.

For a couple of minutes, perhaps longer, Gozo didn't dare to move. Was Elwood Tucker coming back? Everything was still. The only noise came, as always, from the birds in the trees. What would he find inside? He didn't really want to see.

But he had to go in. Finally, he took the few steps that were needed to go round the corner.

He stopped in the doorway. He couldn't see anyone.

Reluctantly, he took a step inside.

'M-Mr Bartlett' he stammered.

'Gozo?'

'Mr Bartlett? Where are you, Mr Bartlett?'

'Down here.'

Gozo took another cautious step. 'Down where?'

'Down *here*, Gozo!'

'Where's down— Oh, I see what you mean!' cried Gozo in astonishment.

The stone circle in the middle of the floor had disappeared. In its place was a metal grille. And far below the grille, at the bottom of a deep stone pit, Bartlett and Jacques le Grand were looking up at him.

They had been sitting with Elwood Tucker in the middle of the room. Then Elwood had got up and gone towards the wall, near the door. A second later, the stone circle dropped away, carrying them with it, and the grille slid out and closed above their heads. They didn't see how he had done it. It was all over in an instant. They didn't have a chance.

'Go over to the wall,' Bartlett called up to Gozo. 'There must be some kind of lever there. See if you can find it.'

Gozo went and looked at the wall around the doorway. There was no sign of a lever.

'I can't find anything, Mr Bartlett.'

'Look harder.'

Gozo looked again. He began to press on the wall, hoping that he might release a lever that he couldn't see. Then he stamped on the ground as well, jumping all around the doorway and then back to the pit in the middle of the room, in case there was a trigger under-foot.

'I'm sorry, Mr Bartlett,' he said eventually, 'I can't find anything. I really can't.' He got down on his knees and tried to lift the grille. 'And I can't . . . *move* . . . *this thing* . . . *either*!' he said, going red with effort.

Jacques raised an eyebrow.

The wall of the pit was smooth and sheer, constructed with the careful workmanship that characterised all the buildings of Run. It couldn't be climbed. And with such workmanship, Bartlett knew, if a lever was hidden somewhere in the walls or floor of the room above, it would be almost impossible to find if you didn't know precisely where to look.

'What are we going to do?' said Gozo.

Bartlett thought. 'We'll have to find someone to let us out. There must be *someone* else who knows how to open this thing.'

'Must there?' said Gozo hopefully.

No, thought Bartlett, not necessarily. But it wasn't impossible. 'Go and get Pfister,' he said. 'Let's see if he can help us.'

'Where is he?'

'I don't know, Gozo. You'll have to find him.'

21

Boas, the carpenter, said he'd seen Pfister heading for the cotton spinners. Apparently he'd promised to help them grease their wheels. Gozo ran to the spinnery. No, said the spinners, they hadn't seen Pfister. They thought he might have promised to bring corn flour to the bakers. He ran to the bakery. Pfister? *Pfister?* No, Pfister hadn't appeared. He'd only promised to bring them corn flour, hadn't he? He'd only told them he'd never, *never* let them down again. So why should they expect that, just once, he'd actually do what he promised? Why should anyone expect— Where *was* he then? Well, he was probably at the spinnery. But Gozo had just *been* to the spinnery! What about the roastery? Gozo ran off again . . .

He bumped into Muss. He wasn't really sure whether he should tell Muss what had happened, but he blurted it out after about ten seconds anyway. He couldn't stop himself. At first Muss didn't believe him. Why would Elwood Tucker throw Bartlett and Jacques down the bottom of a hole? Gozo didn't know.

But Gozo knew one thing—if it were *him* at the bottom of that hole, Bartlett and Jacques wouldn't rest until they'd released him. When he had been locked up in the Pasha's palace, with nothing to do but eat marzipan and cream all day, and it seemed as if there was no way to get him out, they had still managed to rescue him. It had taken weeks, but nothing could stop them.

They had gone *twice* to the City of Flames in order to do it.

'Maybe Elwood has a good reason,' said Muss.

Gozo stared at him in horror. 'A good reason to lock them up? Bartlett and Jacques? What are you talking about?'

Gozo felt a surge of determination. Suddenly, the fact that Bartlett and Jacques had been talking about leaving Run before the Crow Tournament wasn't important at all. What did something like that matter? They needed his help. Inventiveness, Desperation and Perseverance! He was an explorer, wasn't he? Now was the time to prove it. Besides, he'd wanted an adventure. Here it was!

'I'll tell you what I *do* know, Muss. I'm going to get them out.'

'I'm not sure, Gozo,' said Muss, shaking his head thoughtfully. 'There *may* be a reason, you know. You don't want to do anything against Elwood Tucker. You'll regret it. Apart from the Falla, Elwood's the most—' Muss stopped.

'Are you coming with me or not?' demanded Gozo.

Muss grinned. 'Of course I am.'

Eventually, after they had raced over half of Run, they found Pfister. He was with the leatherworkers, stitching WallBalls.

'Pfister, you've got to help!' cried Gozo.

Pfister slapped his forehead. 'I *knew* I'd forgotten something. I promised to help you, didn't I?'

'Not yet,' said Muss, 'but there's the bakers, the spinners, the roasters, the harvesters, the turkey-keepers . . .'

'Pfister! Pfister!' cried Gozo. 'You've got to help. You'll never guess what's happened to Mr Bartlett and Jacques le Grand. They've been—'

'Don't want to know,' said Pfister abruptly.

'But they've been locked up!'

Pfister shrugged. 'None of my business.' He turned around on his stool, and went on with his stitching.

'But Pfister, you don't understand,' said Gozo. 'It's true. They've been *locked up*.'

Pfister shook his head, gazing very closely at the needle in his hand.

'Pfister, come on! This is serious. We're not joking.'

Still Pfister didn't reply.

'Pfister?' said Muss quietly.

Suddenly Pfister turned to face them again. 'I'm sorry. I can't help. I just can't help!' He shook his head, his expression was troubled. 'And you, Muss, if you know what's good for you, stay out of it as well!'

They trudged back to the Circle House.

'Elwood Tucker must have told him not to interfere,' said Muss. 'What other explanation is there? Pfister wouldn't ignore us otherwise, but he'll do anything Elwood says. Most people in Run would.'

'What about you, Muss? He told you to stay out of it as well.'

Muss nodded.

'Muss, I don't want you to get into trouble,' said Gozo. 'Maybe you shouldn't come with me.'

But Muss kept walking with Gozo. He was thinking about it. Eventually he grinned. 'That was just Pfister,' he said. 'No one listens to Pfister.'

'But he warned you, Muss.'

'Did he? I can't remember.'

'Muss, it's no use pretending. He warned you, and he'll tell Elwood Tucker that he did.'

'Well, if Elwood Tucker wants to warn me, he'd better do it himself!' declared Muss, and he folded his small arms defiantly across his chest, striding out along the track with the longest steps that his short legs could produce.

Nothing had changed at the Circle House when they got back. Bartlett and Jacques were still at the bottom of the pit, and the grille was still in place above them.

'I've brought Muss,' said Gozo.

'Hello, Muss,' said Bartlett, craning his head to look up. Jacques le Grand nodded in greeting.

'Is it cold down there?' said Muss.

'No, it's quite pleasant.'

'Are you hungry?'

'Not yet. What about you, Jacques?'

Jacques shook his head.

'We're comfortable for the moment, Muss. Thanks for asking.' Bartlett looked at Gozo. 'Where's Pfister? Couldn't you find him?'

'Oh, I found him.'

'Is he on his way?'

'He said it wasn't any of his business, Mr Bartlett.'

'Did you tell him what happened?'

'He said he couldn't help. Muss thinks Elwood Tucker told him to stay out of it,' Gozo explained. 'Pfister told Muss to stay out of it as well, but Muss doesn't care, and Elwood Tucker can warn him himself if it's so important.'

'That's right!' said Muss.

Bartlett glanced at Jacques for a moment. Then he looked back up at the two boys on top of the grille.

'Do you know anything about this trap, Muss? Do you know how it works?'

Muss shook his head.

'Does anyone, I mean, anyone apart from Elwood Tucker?'

Muss shrugged.

Bartlett sat down with his back against the wall of the well. He frowned in thought. Eventually he looked up again.

'What about the Falla?'

'The Falla?' said Muss. 'I hadn't thought of that.'

'*He'd* know, wouldn't he?'

'Maybe. But it must be the Falla who wants to keep you in here,' said Muss. 'Why else would Elwood Tucker have done it? I told Gozo he probably had a reason, and that's probably it. Now, why would the Falla want you in here?'

'Muss,' said Bartlett, 'when was the last time you actually saw the Falla?'

Muss frowned.

'Muss?'

'I'm thinking, Mr Bartlett.'

Bartlett glanced at Jacques. Jacques nodded.

'Muss,' said Bartlett, 'have you ever actually *seen* the Falla . . . or is it always Elwood Tucker who lets everyone know what he wants?'

Muss didn't reply. Bartlett and Jacques knew the answer anyway.

'All right, listen,' said Bartlett. 'I think there's a good chance the Falla doesn't know anything about what Elwood has done. I think, if you can manage to tell him about it, there's a good chance he'll get us out of here.'

'Well, as long as it's a *good* chance . . .' said Gozo.

'Gozo, it's our *only* chance.'

Then it had better be a good one, thought Gozo.

'Gozo, this is something you're going to have to do yourself. It's going to take all those things we've always talked about, Inventiveness, Desperation and Persev—'

'I know, Mr Bartlett. I already realised that.'

Jacques raised an eyebrow.

'Of course you know,' said Bartlett. He raised a finger in the air. 'Inventiveness!' he cried enthusiastically. 'How do we let the Falla know what's happened? Think! Think! How do we get to him without Elwood Tucker knowing?'

'That's easy,' said Muss.

Everyone looked at him.

'There's one person who can do that whenever she wants: Anya.'

'Anya?' said Bartlett.

'The girl who plays the flute,' said Gozo.

'She's the Falla's daughter,' explained Muss.

Gozo stared at him in surprise.

'Why will she help us?' asked Bartlett.

Muss grinned. 'She'll help Gozo,' he said.

'Why?'

'Because she likes him.'

'She does *not!*' muttered Gozo, turning red and punching Muss on the shoulder.

Bartlett and Jacques tried not to laugh. This was serious!

'Gozo,' said Bartlett, 'just go and talk to her. See if she'll— Gozo? Gozo, what's wrong?'

Gozo wasn't red any more. The blood had drained out of his face. Now he was as white as chalk.

'T-talk to her, Mr Bartlett?' he stammered. 'Me?'

'Desperation, Gozo!' cried Bartlett, jumping to his feet and waving his arm grandly. 'Desperation isn't only about swimming a raging torrent at the height of a storm, or hanging on to a clifftop as an avalanche roars down the slope beneath you. No, it can be anything. Anything that's difficult and testing. It means being Desperate enough to overcome fear, even if it's fear of . . . talking to a girl.'

Jacques nodded, struggling to keep a straight face.

Gozo stared down at the two explorers suspiciously. 'You're not making fun of me, are you, Mr Bartlett?'

'Fun? Me?'

'Jacques?'

Jacques shook his head solemnly.

Gozo stared at them a moment longer.

'All right,' he said suddenly. 'I'll do it! I will. I'm Desperate enough! Don't worry, Mr Bartlett. I'll be back. And before I come back,' he announced, throwing his arm grandly into the air, just as grandly as Bartlett had done, 'I'll make sure the Falla knows!'

And Gozo turned, followed by Muss, and marched proudly out of the house.

Bartlett and Jacques glanced at each other. First a smile crept over Bartlett's lips, and then Jacques began to grin, and a moment later they both burst into uncontrollable laughter. They collapsed on the floor, knees in the air, tears pouring out of their eyes.

'That's funny,' said Gozo, and he stopped outside, on the track that led away from the Circle House. 'Can you hear something, Muss?'

'What?'

'Sounds like . . . someone's in pain.'

'No, it's just birds, they often shriek like that around here,' said Muss, and he hurried him away.

At the bottom of the pit in the Circle House, the two explorers finally stopped laughing. They lay on their backs. Above them, the bars of the grille were thick and heavy. In reality, the situation wasn't particularly amusing.

Jacques looked at Bartlett.

'I know. I know, Jacques. I'd never have thought our fate would depend on Gozo. If you'd asked me before, I'd have been scared to death. But the funny thing is, now that it's happened, I'm not.'

168

Jacques raised an eyebrow.

Bartlett couldn't help grinning again. 'We'll know soon enough. If he can bring himself to talk to that girl, Jacques, he can do *anything*!'

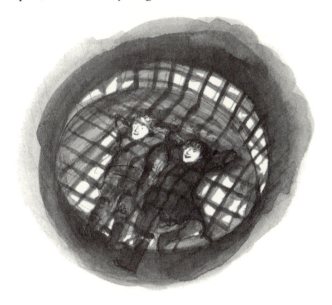

22

Muss and Gozo headed for the HoneyCone. If there was any place where they were likely to find Anya, it was there.

For a while they walked in silence. Gozo was thinking about Anya. 'Why didn't you tell me she was the Falla's daughter?' he demanded eventually. 'No one told me.'

'What difference does it make?' said Muss.

It did make a difference. Gozo wasn't sure what it was. Somehow . . . it made everything harder.

'You shouldn't have told me,' Gozo decided.

Muss shook his head. He wished Gozo would make up his mind. One minute Gozo wanted to know why he hadn't told him earlier, the next minute he didn't want to know at all!

'What's so inventive about talking to her, anyway?' said Muss. He shook his head again. After all the stories Gozo had told him about Bartlett and Jacques le Grand, and all the clever things they thought of, he was quite disappointed that such a simple solution could satisfy the great explorers. 'Anyone could have thought of it. *I* thought of it. It's obvious. If you want to see someone, their daughter should be able to help you.'

'Of course it's obvious,' said Gozo, 'that's the whole point.'

'Why?' said Muss.

It was hard to say. Gozo knew, of course, but the

reason wasn't so easy to put into words without making it sound ridiculous. When you thought about them afterwards, the most Inventive things often were the most obvious. In reality, the most Inventive part usually turned out to be the fact that you thought of them before everyone else realised just how obvious they were.

'Well, if that's all the inventiveness you need to be an explorer . . .' muttered Muss. 'It's not as inventive as WallBall, that's all I can say.'

Not as inventive as WallBall! That was the most ridiculous thing Gozo had ever heard. Muss didn't know the first thing about exploring. He'd never even been out of the forest.

Gozo glanced at Muss. 'I can't believe you've never seen the Falla,' he said, and he shook his head, as if this were the most extraordinary deficiency he had ever heard of.

'I didn't say I'd *never* seen him. I just said . . . I wasn't sure, that's all.'

'*I've* seen him.'

Muss looked at Gozo sharply. 'Really, have you?'

Gozo nodded. That had done the trick! He could see that Muss was impressed with *that*. Gozo sauntered along the path, as if it were perfectly normal for a boy like him to see the Falla every day of the week.

'When did you see him?'

'On the day I arrived.'

'What's he like?' said Muss eagerly.

'He's fat.'

'Really?'

'As fat as can be. As fat as a bear. As fat as a hippopotamus. As fat as a . . . a . . .'

'What?' said Muss.

Gozo frowned. It was much easier to think of the right word when there was someone like Bartlett to tell him which word he was thinking of. 'As fat as a . . . *tree*!'

Gozo stole a glance at Muss, to see what effect this was having on him. 'As fat as a tree' hadn't sounded as astonishing as he had hoped. Yet Muss looked even more impressed than before.

'Is he the fattest person you've ever seen?' asked Muss.

'Easily,' said Gozo. 'As fat as the *two* fattest people I've ever seen, put together.'

Muss shook his head in disbelief.

'You should see him,' said Gozo.

'Yes,' said Muss, 'I should.'

'Don't worry,' Gozo reassured him. 'When I speak to the Falla, I'll make sure to mention your name. I won't forget you, Muss, even though I *will* be talking to the Falla, of course, and very few people, it seems, ever get to do that. But you can count on me. I'll just say to him, "Falla, there's one person I think you should meet. His name's Muss." Of course, I may need to convince him, because he may not understand immediately why he ought to meet you—because, after all, you're just one of the boys here, and Muss is a bit of a strange name, which I'm sure you know already—so I'll just say to him, "Falla, don't think I'm just saying that. You really must meet Muss, because . . ."' Gozo paused. 'Why, Muss? Can you think of any reason I can give him?'

'Because . . . I've never seen him before?'

Gozo shook his head. 'Lots of people haven't seen him before.'

'Because . . . I've thought of a new rule for WallBall?'

'Have you?'

'Yes, but I'm not telling anyone, or they'll take credit for it. I'm only going to tell the Falla.'

'Well . . .' said Gozo. He considered this interesting piece of news as they moved along the path. 'How do I know this rule's really good?' he asked at last. 'I can't go telling the Falla he should meet you if I'm not certain it's a good one. You'd better tell me what your new rule is, Muss.'

'I'm not telling *anyone*, Gozo.'

'Then I don't think I can use it as a reason for the Falla to meet you, Muss,' said Gozo regretfully, 'not if you're not prepared to tell me.'

Muss frowned. 'I really shouldn't tell you, Gozo.'

Gozo sighed. 'I can't help you, then. When the Falla says "Tell me about Muss. Why should I meet him?", I'm just going to have to say, "Well, Muss claims to have invented a new rule for WallBall, but no one knows what it is or if it's any good." I can't lie to the Falla, Muss. I'm sure you understand.'

Muss nodded.

'So are you going to tell me? Yes or no?'

Muss sighed. '*If* I tell you, Gozo, will you promise—'

Muss stopped. Gozo turned as white as chalk.

In front of them, at the end of the path, was the pale wall of the HoneyCone. And already they could hear, very faintly, a familiar sound coming from its direction.

173

Anya was sitting outside Grandma Myrtle's workroom. She took her flute from her lips, and her soft brown eyes looked directly into Gozo's.

She *was* the most beautiful girl in the world, Gozo thought, and he could hardly breathe. She was the most beautiful girl, and the cleverest and the most talented, and she could play a flute and *he* couldn't even play WallBall without giving away penalties right in front of the goals.

Muss nudged him. But Gozo's feet had turned into blocks of lead, and the muscles of his face had turned into solid sheets of stone, and the only reason he knew he was even alive was because of his heart, which was thumping inside his chest as if someone were pounding on it like a drum.

The girl waited. The seconds passed, and to Gozo they seemed like hours. Desperation, he stammered to himself, Desperation. Where *was* his Desperation? He had left it on the path, it seemed, used it up telling Muss ridiculous stories, which he didn't even believe himself, about what he would do when he met the Falla.

Eventually Muss got tired of waiting for him. 'Anya,

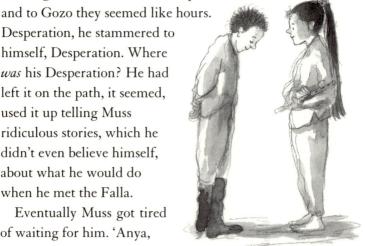

Gozo wants to speak to you,' he informed her.

Anya nodded inquisitively. Gozo stared back in terror. How was Muss able to talk to her, just like that, just as if she were a normal human being and not the most beautiful, talented, clever . . .

Anya smiled.

Muss smiled as well. He nudged Gozo. Then he started to push him. 'He does. He really wants to talk to you, Anya.'

Finally Gozo was standing right in front of her. She looked up at him, and then she patted the stone beside her, as if inviting him to sit.

Muss pushed down on his shoulders.

Gozo felt foolish and clumsy. She was so slim and agile. He stared down at his boots. She was barefoot. She must be thinking, he thought, what a clumsy oaf he was.

Somehow he found himself on the stone, sitting next to her.

'What do you want to talk to me about?' she asked.

Gozo's heart thumped harder than ever. Her voice was quiet, so soft it could have been a series of notes coming gently from her flute.

'Gozo?'

The sound of his name, from her lips, warmed him like a finger of sunlight pointing through a cloudy sky. No one, he felt, had ever said his name like that before.

He looked up at her. She had that inquisitive look on her face again. Then she smiled once more. Before he knew it, he had smiled back at her!

She laughed. Her teeth were white. He thought again,

how beautiful she was. But this time, for some reason, it didn't make him freeze.

'My two friends . . .' he began.

'Congratulations! It's about time,' muttered Muss.

Gozo glanced up at him angrily. Then he turned back to Anya and started again. 'My two friends, Bartlett and Jacques, they're in a kind of prison. I mean, they're in a cage. No, what I mean is, they're in a hole.'

'What he really means is they're in a pit in the Circle House,' said Muss.

Anya was frowning, trying to understand.

'Someone's locked them in a hole. Elwood Tucker. He's the one who's locked them in.'

'Why?' murmured Anya.

'That's what I said,' remarked Muss. 'Why? He could have a good reason, Gozo. It's possible.'

'He *doesn't* have a good reason!' retorted Gozo. He turned back to Anya. 'I don't know why Elwood Tucker did it. I don't know. I don't know why, or what he's planning to do, or whether he'll ever let them out. They're my friends and now they're locked up in a hole and . . . and . . .'

Suddenly Gozo felt he was going to cry. He fought and fought against the tears. That would be the worst thing, the last straw, to cry in front of this girl. What would she think of him?

'You see, *I* said the Falla must have told him to do it,' Muss explained. 'But Bartlett said the Falla doesn't know—mightn't know—but really, what's the chance of that? It's ridiculous, isn't it? How could Elwood Tucker do something like this without your father knowing, Anya? I told them, of course, but Bartlett wanted us to talk to the Falla. Talk to the Falla? It is, it's ridiculous, isn't it? We're wasting your time, I know. But Bartlett insisted. And he *is* at the bottom of a pit, with Jacques le Grand, and when a man at the bottom of a pit insists, you feel at least you ought to try. So here we are, and now that we've asked you, and you can see how ridiculous it is, we don't need to waste any more of your time . . .'

Gozo wished Muss would be quiet. He wasn't helping.

'He *doesn't* know,' said Anya.

Muss and Gozo stared at her.

'He doesn't know?' whispered Muss.

But Anya was looking at Gozo. 'Your friend's right. I think you should talk to my father.'

23

The entrance to the Falla's house was not simple. Its passages were like a maze. Although it wasn't the largest building in Run, the Falla's house was one of the most complicated, and what it had originally been used for, no one knew. On one side of the building, at ground level, there were three doorways cut into the stone. From two of them, passages ended blindly after a couple of turns. From the other doorway, the passage turned, dipped down a flight of stairs so that it was actually underground, turned, turned, and turned again, going far out from the walls of the building and under the forest before twisting back, then rose, still swerving and branching, through the heart of the building, until it came out into a room in the middle of the structure on top of the platform. But as it turned under the forest and then rose through the building, there were false branches, blind passages that turned and branched in turn before they ended . . . and you could imagine that a person who was lost within them might never find his way out alive.

But Anya knew her way. Before they went in, she told them to be silent. She carried a torch for light, and led Gozo and Muss, wide-eyed and fearful, through the dark passages of the maze.

And then they came out into a bright room at the top. The ceiling was punctured by a single circular hole that was open to the sky, like the pupil of a gigantic eye through which sunlight streamed.

Anya put a finger to her lips. The room had four doors, one in each wall. Very quietly, she opened one of them and went into a short corridor that ended at another door. But almost at once she heard voices beyond it.

Hurriedly, Anya turned back. In the central room, she opened another of the doors, and took Gozo and Muss down a long curving corridor that ended at a kitchen. Here there was a big fireplace, over which hung a set of pots. A row of enormous vats stood against one wall, and a stack of chests stood in a corner. Another wall was taken up with a series of three ovens. The fireplace was cold and the pots were empty. There was still some warmth coming from the ovens, but they were cooling. Everything was very clean and tidy. Obviously, someone had finished cooking not long before. And if there was any doubt, the table in the middle of the kitchen proved it! The table was covered with food. There were dishes of cakes and savoury dumplings, bowls of desserts, beakers of sauces, and platters of pies and pasties.

Still in silence, Anya went to the wall where the vats stood. Here, at about chest height, there was a pair of small doors, through which dishes could be passed to the next room. Through the crack between the doors the voices could be heard again, more clearly than before.

Gozo recognised Elwood Tucker's voice.

'I've told you, you don't want to see them. They're settling in. It would only disturb them.'

'Why don't you want me to see them?'

'I didn't say I don't want you to see them. Did I ever say that, Falla?'

At the mention of the Falla's name, Muss' eyes went wide. Gozo listened intently. He reached out for a cake from the table and began to nibble it as the voices continued.

'Remember, I know what they're like. *I* know how to handle them. What would you say? Have you thought about it yet? You'd frighten them off.'

'Would I?'

'At this very moment, Bartlett's out there with the twins, and Jacques . . . I don't know, he's doing something strong. He likes doing strong things. He might be throwing rocks around.'

'So they're still . . . free?'

'Free? What do you mean, Falla? Of course they're free.'

There was silence for a moment. Then the Falla laughed. Even through the doors, you could hear the relief in his voice. 'They're simple chaps, aren't they?'

'Very simple!'

Now both men were laughing. Gozo was so angry he could have leapt straight through those doors and landed right on Elwood Tucker's head—and he might have done it, if Anya hadn't caught his eye, and held up a finger sternly, to tell him to wait.

'What about the third one? Wasn't there a third one?' said the Falla's voice.

'Him? Oh, I don't know what he's up to. Probably playing WallBall. That's enough to keep him happy. He's only a boy, Falla. He can't do anything by himself.'

Muss turned to Gozo and grinned. Very funny, thought Gozo. Can't do anything by himself? Well, Elwood Tucker was making a big mistake!

'I don't know what I'd do without you, Elwood.'

'I know, Falla.'

'You're my eyes and ears. I should go out and see things for myself . . . but it's difficult nowadays. It wasn't always like this. Do you know, Elwood, when I was young, I was as skinny as a sapling? Have I ever told you that, Elwood?'

'Yes, Falla.'

'Yes. Well, that was long before you came. By the time you came, I was already a grand old oak.'

'Very grand, Falla.'

'And I keep getting grander!'

The Falla laughed. Elwood Tucker joined in.

'You're my eyes, Elwood. You know you are. You're my eyes and ears.'

'Then I should go and use them.'

'Yes, Elwood. Go. Go and use them.'

There were footsteps, then the sound of a door closing.

Anya didn't move. Gozo and Muss watched her. She was waiting until she was sure it would be safe to go to her father's room. Elwood Tucker might have forgotten something, for instance, and might turn back, or he might stop for a moment before he left the building, or . . .

Behind them, the door of the kitchen opened.

'What are you doing here?'

Gozo spun round in terror.

But it wasn't Elwood Tucker. It was a short, stout man, with close-cropped hair and a head like a bullet. He was wearing a spotless white apron.

'What are you doing in my kitchen? *You!* Put that cake down! Anya, what's going on?'

'We were just waiting, Cook Stubbins.'

'Waiting for what?'

'For you,' said Anya, as calm as a caterpillar. Gozo gazed at her with admiration.

Cook Stubbins frowned. 'Well, here I am,' he said eventually, in a puzzled tone.

'Then we can go,' said Anya, and she began to lead the way out.

'Boy! *Boy!*' shouted Cook Stubbins. Gozo turned around. 'Take the cake. You've eaten half of it. Don't put it back on the plate. Disgusting! That kind of thing isn't done in my kitchen.'

Gozo went back to the table and gingerly retrieved the part-nibbled cake. Why did Cook Stubbins have to shout like that? Couldn't he have taken him aside, for example, and whispered? Gozo could feel Anya's eyes on him. He wished he'd never touched that cake in the first place!

The Falla was lying on his couch. He looked around when he heard the door open.

'Anya!' he said with delight. But then he frowned, seeing Gozo and Muss following her. 'There are two boys with you, Anya,' he said, as if his daughter might not be aware of it.

'They need to talk to you,' said Anya, and then she sat down on the couch opposite her father, where Elwood Tucker had been sitting before, and that was the last thing she said.

The Falla turned his gaze on them. 'Not accustomed to talking to boys . . .' he muttered to himself. 'Well?' he demanded impatiently, as if he had somewhere very important to go, although, in reality, he had no intention of getting off his couch.

Gozo coughed. 'I'm Gozo,' he muttered.

'What's that? Can't hear you, boy!' said the Falla. He reached out towards a plate of sweets, and took one, and began to munch it very quickly, not taking his eyes off Gozo.

'I'm Gozo,' said Gozo, more loudly. 'I came with . . . you know, Bartlett and Jacques le Grand.'

'Of course,' said the Falla, 'I recognise you now. You're the third one, aren't you? And what about *you*, boy? I can't remember a fourth.'

Now, for a change, it was Muss who was struck dumb. Here he was, finally—*the Falla*! And he really was the fattest man in the world. He was as fat as . . . as fat as . . . there was nothing Muss had ever seen that he could even use for comparison.

'This is Muss,' said Gozo, discovering that sometimes it's easier to talk for another person than for oneself. 'He didn't come with us. He's from Run. He invents new rules for WallBall.'

Muss whispered in Gozo's ear.

'One rule, Falla. He's invented one new rule. But I'm sure he could invent more if he tried.'

'Really?'

Gozo nodded. Muss didn't look sure.

'Anya, why have you brought these boys here?' said the Falla. 'I'm very tired. It must be time for my nap.'

Gozo looked around to see what Anya would say. But she didn't say anything. She just nodded at Gozo, as if to tell him that he shouldn't worry about her father's nap, and he should say what he had to say.

Gozo turned back to the Falla. Now that he faced him, and had reminded him who he was, Gozo didn't know quite how to go on. He didn't want to make that huge man on the couch angry. It was a frightening thought. But he had to say something! The longer he stood there without speaking, he could see, the more impatient the Falla was growing. At last Gozo came to the conclusion which everyone, sooner or later, reaches in such a situation: that the only way to say what you have to say . . . is to say it, the plainer the better.

Gozo glanced at Anya once more. Then he took a deep breath. He thought of Bartlett and Jacques at the bottom of that pit, to remind himself why he was there, to give himself the Desperation to go on.

'Falla, Elwood Tucker's lying to you.'

The Falla's expression didn't change. He didn't even blink.

'Falla, I said that Elwood—'

'I heard what you said.' The Falla watched him steadily.

Gozo didn't know what to say. It was as if the air had suddenly become so heavy, so cold, that he could barely breathe it.

'Explain yourself.'

Gozo thought about the lies he had just heard Elwood Tucker tell. He thought about Bartlett and Jacques again, he *made* himself concentrate on that, think about them locked at the bottom of the pit.

'Explain yourself!'

'He's locked them up,' Gozo blurted out.

'Who?'

'Bartlett and Jacques. My friends. Elwood Tucker has locked them up.'

'What are you talking about?'

'He's locked them up.'

'Nonsense,' said the Falla. 'At this very moment, they're chopping trees and . . . and throwing rocks.'

185

'No they're not. They're at the bottom of a pit, in a great big hole.'

'Where? Where is this *pit*?'

'In the Circle House.'

Now, only now, did the Falla's expression begin to change. He peered closely at Gozo.

'Have you seen them?'

'Yes.'

'What does this pit look like?'

What did any pit look like? 'It's deep,' said Gozo. 'And it's all made out of stone. And there's a metal cage at the top.'

'Have *you* seen them, Anya?' said the Falla, turning to his daughter.

'I have,' said Muss.

'You went to the Circle House? What were you doing there?'

'I went there with Gozo.'

'What's your name again?'

'Muss.'

'Stupid name. I don't believe you.' The Falla looked back at Gozo. 'I don't believe *you*, either.'

'It's true,' said Gozo.

'I've known Elwood Tucker for ten years,' said the Falla. 'And I've known you for ten minutes. Why should I believe you?'

'Because it's true!' cried Gozo, who was so angry at Elwood Tucker's lies and the unfairness of what he had done to Bartlett and Jacques that, at least for a moment, he had forgotten how frightening it would be to anger

186

the huge man on the couch. 'It's true, that's why. And when something's true, it doesn't matter who says it, if you've known them for ten years or ten minutes, if they're forty years old or fourteen. If it's true, its true! And if you're any kind of a Falla, you shouldn't need me to tell you!'

Gozo finished his speech and crossed his arms emphatically. The Falla glanced at his daughter and noticed how she was gazing at Gozo. It was lucky Gozo couldn't see her. He would have been too tongue-tied to say another word.

Now something began to happen. The Falla started to raise himself on the couch. Gradually, he sat up. Gozo and Muss watched the lengthy operation anxiously, wondering whether he would succeed.

'Bring me Pfister,' said the Falla eventually. 'Elwood said Pfister's been looking after them. I'll ask him.'

'Pfister won't tell you the truth,' said Gozo. 'Pfister will tell you whatever Elwood Tucker wants him to tell.'

'Then who *can* I believe?' cried the Falla. 'Elwood's my eyes, my ears!'

'You'll have to use your own,' said Gozo.

The Falla looked at him. 'You're very clever for such a young man,' he said.

Gozo stared at him in astonishment, wondering whether *he* was the young man the Falla was talking about.

The Falla shook his head. 'They're in the Circle House, you say?'

Gozo nodded.

'And you've seen the pit yourself? Tell me again, what does it look like?'

Gozo told him.

The Falla sighed. 'That's the one.' He shook his head, muttering to himself. 'I should have known it. I did. I did know it. Why pretend?'

Gozo glanced at Muss. The other boy shrugged.

'And now, if I can't trust Elwood . . . I'll have to go there myself. I'll just have to do it. There's no alternative. There's just no alternative at all.' The Falla looked around, as if he were hoping that someone would say that there was.

But no one replied, because there wasn't.

The Falla began to rise to his feet. This was just as slow an operation as his previous effort, but even more staggering. The idea of that huge bulk falling flat on its face was something no one in that room wanted to imagine.

'Look at me!' cried the Falla. 'I can barely stand. I can barely walk. How can I get there?'

'Inventiveness!' cried Gozo enthusiastically, raising a finger in the air.

Everyone looked at him in puzzlement. It always sounded so impressive, thought Gozo, when Bartlett said it.

They were still waiting. The Falla, Muss, Anya.

'I mean, well, we'll think of something,' explained Gozo. 'Something always turns up.'

'Not always,' said Muss.

24

'We'll just carry him' said Muss. 'Look at Grandma Myrtle. Whenever she wants to go anywhere, someone just picks her up and carries her.'

'Grandma Myrtle's as light as a chicken,' said Gozo. 'Who's going to carry the Falla? You, Muss? Are *you* going to carry him?'

Muss didn't reply. They were standing outside the Falla's house. Anya had brought them out through the twisting tunnels, and now they were in the sunlight once more.

'You see?' said Gozo. 'Inventiveness *isn't* so easy, is it? Now you understand. Mr Bartlett's the most Inventive man I've ever met. I've told you before, when we had to go to get the melidrop for the Queen, he went on an ice voyage to do it. And when we had to bring the sun to the City of Flames, which is underground, he worked out how to do that as well!'

'I still don't believe anyone could do that,' objected Muss. 'Bring the sun underground? Tell me how he did it!'

Gozo hesitated. Then he leaned over and whispered the solution in his ear.

Muss' eyes went wide. 'That *is* inventive,' he said, and he leaned over, in turn, and whispered the answer to Anya.

Anya nodded thoughtfully, and Gozo wondered

whether she might even be a tiny bit impressed with him, just for knowing the answer, even though it was Bartlett who had actually thought of it.

'Well, if we have to find a way of carrying the Falla, what are we doing here?' said Muss. 'Let's go and ask Mr Bartlett.'

'He's not the only one who can be Inventive!' exclaimed Gozo. He glanced at Anya, hoping she knew who he was talking about.

But he couldn't tell what she was thinking. No, she was probably laughing at him, he thought. He concentrated. How could they carry the Falla? How could they carry a big . . . huge . . . enormous *whale* of a man like the Falla of Run?

'I know!' he cried. 'We put him on a chair, and we get a whole lot of other people to help us, and then we all lift the chair . . .'

'Really?' said Muss. 'You'd need ten people. There wouldn't be room for them. They'd knock each other over.'

It was true. You could only get a couple of people around a chair. Gozo frowned. Trust Muss to think of something to spoil his idea!

'Let's just go to Mr Bartlett,' said Muss. 'That really might be the best . . .'

'I know! We put the chair on *wheels*, and we get a whole lot of people to pull it with ropes.'

'And getting it up and down the stairs inside the Falla's house, Gozo? Have you thought about that?'

No, Gozo hadn't thought about that. 'All right, all

right, listen to this! I know what we do for the stairs. We'll get turkeys . . .'

'Turkeys?' said Muss.

Gozo nodded excitedly. 'Turkeys are strong. This is how it works. We get a whole lot of turkeys.'

'Strong turkeys, I suppose?'

'Strong ones, yes. We get a whole lot of strong turkeys and put them in a cage . . . except it's a special cage, without a bottom, so they can walk. See? *Then* we put the chair on *top* of the cage, and we make the turkeys go up and down the stairs . . .'

'You know, I've just had a great idea!' said Muss. 'Why don't we go and ask Mr Bartlett?'

Gozo shook his head angrily at Muss. Maybe the turkey cage wasn't the best idea. And maybe he hadn't completely thought it through yet. But there was a whole building full of the birds, so they could easily experiment until they got it right.

'Poles,' said Anya, who had been thinking quietly while Muss and Gozo were arguing.

'Poles?' said Muss. 'What are you talking about, Anya?'

'All we have to do is put poles under the chair. Then people can carry it in front and behind. That's how we get enough people to lift it.'

Gozo and Muss stared. Then Gozo grinned. 'Inventiveness!' he cried, raising his finger triumphantly in the air. 'Any objections, Mr Muss? Any problems with poles? Still want to go to Mr Bartlett, do you?'

Muss shook his head. 'We'll go to Uncle Boas.'

'Exactly. Boas. Boas will be able to fix it for us. Let's go.'

But Anya didn't move.

'Aren't you coming, Anya?'

'I'll wait here,' she said. And she sat down with her back against the wall, and as Gozo and Muss left, they heard the music from her flute begin to waft into the air.

Poles, thought Gozo to himself as they went to the carpenter. Poles! Why couldn't *he* have thought of that? If only he had thought of it, instead of Anya, she would have thought he was wonderfully clever. It was obvious. It was simple, like all the best ideas. Even Bartlett and Jacques would be impressed. Of course, he *would* tell them who'd thought of it. If you couldn't trust an explorer to tell the truth, as Sutton Pufrock said, you couldn't trust the sun to rise or the rain to fall. No, when he told them about it later, he wouldn't pretend he'd thought of it himself. Of course he wouldn't.

But perhaps Gozo should have been thinking less about what he was going to tell Bartlett and Jacques after he rescued them, and more about all the things that could still go wrong. As Bartlett could have told him, it's one thing to think of an idea—another thing to make it succeed.

Boas the carpenter looked at them suspiciously. They wanted a chair? With poles?

Of course, the carpenter had a chair, he had a number of chairs, and they could have any one of them. He didn't have poles, but he could easily make them. He folded his

arms across his chest. He was a lean, sinewy man, and wore a leather apron without a shirt underneath it, so every time he raised a hammer or drove a saw, you could see the knotty muscles of his arms bunching and tensing. When he crossed his arms, the sheet of muscle below his armpit stood out like a ridge.

'Who's it for?' he said.

Gozo looked at Muss.

'We just need it for something, Uncle Boas,' said Muss.

'What?'

'We need it for . . . for . . .'

'For a performance,' Gozo blurted out.

'What performance?'

What performance? Good question. Gozo looked at Muss anxiously.

'The Crow Performance,' said Muss.

'The Crow Performance?' said Boas, and he dug a finger thoughtfully into his ear. 'We don't use a chair in the Crow Performance.'

'No,' said Muss, 'but I think we're going to.'

Boas didn't look convinced. 'The Crow Festival's next week. This is the first I've heard of a *chair*.'

'Not many people know,' said Muss.

'Three, at the moment,' said Gozo.

'Four now, including you, Uncle Boas,' said Muss.

Boas continued to look at them doubtfully. 'All right,' he said eventually. 'Come back in three days.'

'Three days!' squeaked Gozo.

Boas gave him a sharp glance.

'We need it a bit sooner, Uncle Boas,' said Muss. 'We have to practise.'

'How much sooner?'

'By tonight?'

Boas laughed.

'I know it's a bit of a rush.'

Boas laughed again.

'Really, Uncle Boas. We really, really need it.'

'Really? You really, really need it by tonight. And only three people know about it? And it's for the Crow Performance, where we've never used a chair before? I know people think I'm not very smart, Muss, but you're insulting me. A nephew shouldn't insult his uncle.'

'I'm sorry. I didn't mean to,' said Muss.

'Neither did I,' said Gozo, who wasn't the carpenter's nephew, but didn't think it was very nice to insult someone even if he wasn't your relative.

Boas considered. He screwed up his nose and dug inside his ear again.

'Why won't you tell me why you need it?'

'It's a secret,' said Muss.

'Well, don't make fun of me, Muss. Don't tell me it's for the Crow Performance. If it's a secret, it's a secret.'

'All right, Uncle Boas. It's a secret. And it's not for the Crow Performance.'

'We'd like to tell you, but we can't,' added Gozo.

'Well, that's better. At least you're telling the truth now.' The carpenter peered at them closely. 'No one's going to get into trouble? No one's going to get hurt, are they? Tell me, Muss, honestly.'

Muss shook his head. 'No one's going to get into trouble.'

'Or hurt?'

'Or hurt.'

'Is that the truth?' said Boas.

Muss and Gozo nodded. They certainly hoped no one was going to get hurt!

'By tonight,' Boas murmured to himself, and he looked around his workroom, as if trying to see whether he had the time. The place was ankle-deep in sawdust and wood shavings, and there were half-finished chairs and cupboards and couches and tables all over the place, and Gozo couldn't see what you could tell just by looking at it all. But obviously Boas could, because a moment later he turned back to them and said: 'All right. Since it's you who's asking, Muss, and since you're telling me the truth, I'll do it by tonight. How long should the poles be?'

Muss glanced at Gozo, who shrugged.

'Long enough for two people on each end,' said Muss.

'Better make it three,' said Gozo, thinking of the Falla's size.

'But no longer,' added Muss, thinking of the bends and branchings they would have to negotiate in the passages of the Falla's house.

Boas nodded. 'Come back this evening.'

'Thanks, Uncle Boas,' said Muss. 'And it really is a secret. You can't tell anyone. Don't tell Pfister. Don't even tell Elwood Tucker.'

Boas laughed. 'Don't tell Elwood Tucker . . .'

'I'm serious, Uncle Boas. Please, don't tell anyone.'

'*Especially* Elwood Tucker,' added Gozo.

Boas's eyes narrowed again. 'Muss . . .'

'No one's going to get into trouble, Uncle Boas. I promise you.'

Boas looked at him a moment longer, as if trying to see what his nephew was really thinking. Then he nodded.

Gozo and Muss started to walk away. After a couple of seconds, Boas shouted after them. 'I forgot to ask you, how big is the chair you want?'

'Big,' said Muss.

'The biggest you've got,' added Gozo.

Boas shook his head. 'Three people on each end of the poles? The biggest chair I've got? Whoever you're going to carry must be a real monster!'

'Who said we're carrying anybody?' said Gozo.

The carpenter grinned. 'I told you, I'm not as dumb as people say.'

'Do you think he'll keep it secret?' asked Gozo.

Muss shrugged. 'He said he would. People say Uncle Boas isn't too smart. I don't know about that, but he does what he says.'

'So now we need to get the others.'

Muss nodded. 'Gandel, Bertram, Hardy . . .' he said, counting them off on his fingers.

'Then there's Tam, Laurence, Philp . . . That's six.'

'Eight, with the two of us, Gozo.'

'Eight. Eight should be enough, don't you think?'

Muss shrugged. He didn't know how many people you would need to carry the Falla. How could anyone know how many people you would need to carry someone *that* heavy?

'Well, it'll have to be enough,' muttered Gozo. 'What will we tell them?'

'We'll just tell them to be there. We'll tell them . . . we'll tell them Uncle Boas is making something for the WallBall court, and they all have to be there to help bring it over.'

'No, someone will tell Pfister,' said Gozo. 'Pfister will know it isn't true.'

'We'll tell them they can't tell Pfister. We'll tell them they can't tell anybody.'

'They'll want to know why.'

'We'll think of something!' exclaimed Muss.

Gozo nodded. But he wasn't sure. He began to realise that the most dangerous part of the operation was only beginning. It would take Boas the rest of the day to build the chair. Anyone might just happen to turn up at his workroom and see what he was making, even if he didn't tell them anything about it. In fact, the less he told them, the more curious they'd be. And one of the WallBallers might just happen to mention that was doing something special that evening, without even saying what it was. The less he said, the more people would pry. Soon, Gozo could see, lots of people would know that *something* was going on. And when people know that *something* is going on, it usually doesn't take too long before they try to find out what the *something* is.

And the more people who knew—even if it was only that *something* was going on—the more likely it was that Elwood Tucker would find out. And if Elwood Tucker found out, they were going to be in trouble!

Where was Elwood Tucker? Gozo's stomach knotted whenever he thought of him. The ex-explorer seemed to come and go in Run like a phantom. He was out there somewhere, Gozo knew. When would he appear next? All through the afternoon, as Gozo waited for the carpenter's work to be ready, he had the feeling that Elwood Tucker must be waiting as well, watching, choosing his moment to pounce.

25

It was almost sunset. At the edge of the clearing stood Elwood Tucker. He stared at the Circle House. The white stone of the wall reflected the light.

He walked towards the door.

Inside, Bartlett and Jacques heard someone come in. They looked up hopefully. Tucker's bald head appeared above the grille.

He peered at them. 'Thought someone was coming to let you out, did you?' He shook his head, still gazing at them. Then he said: 'I've brought you some food. You must be getting hungry. Watch out!'

Tucker opened a small hatch in the grille. Bartlett and Jacques scrambled to their feet. Corn bread and cakes fell. A bag followed. Jacques caught a bulging waterskin.

Tucker threw down a bucket as well. 'That's the best I can do for now.'

Bartlett opened the bag. He pulled out a turkey leg and handed it to Jacques, then took another for himself. The two explorers sat down and began to eat.

Tucker closed the hatch. But he didn't leave. He watched them. Bartlett and Jacques knew he was there, but they merely glanced at each other and didn't say a word.

The silence went on for a while, the two explorers chewing, knowing that Elwood was watching them.

'You know, I'm sorry about this,' said Elwood eventually.

Bartlett and Jacques continued to eat.

'It must be awful. I mean, it's humiliating, isn't it? And it's me. *Me* doing it to you. That must be worse than anything.'

Bartlett took some bread. Jacques raised the water-skin, threw back his head, and drank.

'I didn't want to do it. You know that, don't you? You know I didn't want to do it to you.'

Bartlett drank from the waterskin as well.

'*Answer me!*'

Now Bartlett and Jacques looked up. Elwood's eyes were wild.

'Why did you come? Why did you have to do it? Why couldn't you just stay away? Ten years! Isn't that enough time? Couldn't you just have forgotten about me?'

Only now did Bartlett speak, softly, calmly. 'Do you think we were looking for you, Elwood?'

But it was as if Elwood Tucker were no longer capable of hearing Bartlett, Jacques or anything but the voice that was raging inside his own head. His chest heaved. His eyes blazed. 'I dreamt! About you, Bartlett. Nightmares! You'd find me. You'd come for me. You and Jacques. You always thought you were better than me. You'd never let it rest, you'd have to prove it once and for all. You'd have to humiliate me. What did you want? *I* was the best. How many times did I have to prove it? How much longer was I meant to keep going? I gave up. Didn't you realise it? Why can't a man give up?' Elwood was kneeling on the grille now, peering down at them. He laughed madly. 'I was so frightened that I'd give up, that I *gave up*! Don't you understand? Can't you see? How else could it end? It was the only way out.'

Now he was silent.

'No one's trying to prove anything,' said Bartlett quietly.

'Of *course* you are. We were rivals, Bartlett. Don't you remember? Rivals in everything.'

'We were friends, as well.'

'Friends? *Friends?* You were out to beat me. You had the Reliability . . . No, what is it? The Patience . . . No, the Perseverance. That's it. Didn't you? So proud of your Perseverance. Well, I was the more Inventive, I was the more Desperate. Do you deny it?'

Bartlett shook his head.

'Of course you wouldn't deny it. Not from down there. But if I let you out, it will be just like before.'

'Just like what, Elwood?'

Elwood Tucker laughed, throwing a sly glance at the explorers below him.

Bartlett looked at Jacques. Jacques shook his head. Was Elwood mad? He had been their rival, it was true, but that was when they had been younger. He was talking as if they were still boys. The world was vast, with more places than any one person could hope to explore in his entire lifetime. There was room for more than one great explorer. What mattered was the exploits *you* accomplished, not whether somebody else achieved something harder or easier. Surely now, after all these years, Elwood Tucker didn't think they begrudged him his successes.

'Elwood, as a matter of interest,' said Bartlett, '*did* you explore this forest?'

'What was that?' said Tucker sharply.

'Did you stop here on your way in or on your way out?'

Elwood grinned, as if he understood what Bartlett was *really* asking. 'What do you *think*? I explored it. Do you imagine I was starving? Did you really believe that story? I'd been all the way to the coast, sailed down the river on a raft I built myself. Then I decided to come back on foot, explore the whole forest once and for all. I could have survived for months. You'll never be able to say you were the first, Bartlett!'

'No, you were the first, Elwood.'

'First again!' retorted Tucker smugly. 'You haven't explored it, have you? You were on your way in! Well, you don't need to bother. There's nothing else here. All the way to the coast and back, nothing but forest. The only thing here is Run. I could have missed it completely, you know, I could have walked right past it. But of course I was too good an explorer to do that.'

'Other explorers would like to know,' said Bartlett. 'They'd like to know there's nothing here. It'll save them a lot of effort. And they'd like to know you succeeded, Elwood. Sutton Pufrock would. It would make him proud. He thinks you died trying.'

'And you'll tell him, I suppose,' said Elwood Tucker with a sneer.

'Yes,' said Bartlett, 'we'll tell him.'

Elwood Tucker gazed at them. The sun was setting now, and the light in the house was failing rapidly. Bartlett could just make out Elwood Tucker's features above the grille.

'Elwood,' said Bartlett, 'what are you doing? This isn't right. Let us out. We travelled together, we explored together. We were rivals, but we were friends. Don't you remember? We helped each other. Remember that day on the Piuong Glacier?'

'Be quiet!'

'Do you remember the overhang? The one where Sutton Pufrock fell? Remember how we climbed down to rescue him? We've been back there, Jacques and I. We thought about you that day, Elwood. Not only that day. We've thought about you a lot.'

'*Be quiet!*' roared Elwood Tucker.

Now Bartlett couldn't see him at all, he could only hear his voice. 'Elwood,' he said, 'this is crazy. How will it end?'

Bartlett and Jacques heard footsteps leaving the house.

'Elwood? *Elwood?*'

There was no answer. Where Elwood Tucker had gone, they had no idea.

'You know what he needs, don't you?'

'He needs to stop thinking he was so great,' muttered Jacques. 'He was a good explorer. So? We're good as well.'

'That's not what I meant,' said Bartlett. He lit a candle. It had been standing in the middle of the stone circle when Elwood Tucker had locked them in, and had plunged to the bottom with them.

'Save it,' said Jacques, as the flame sputtered to life.

'No. I want to read you something.'

Bartlett took a small book out of his pocket. It was the book of poems that had been given to him by the Ahsap of the City of Flames, after he had brought them the sun. The Ahsap was a slim man with a thoughtful face, and he was more comfortable with ideas than with action. Most of the poems in the book were a bit absurd, and they made Bartlett laugh, which is why he liked to read them. But inside the absurdity of the poems, if you looked for it, you would usually find a certain idea, or the seed of an unusual wisdom. That was probably why the Ahsap wrote them. It had taken Bartlett a while to understand this, and the book had become one of his most prized possessions, more important than any jewels or treasure given to him over the years as a reward for his exploits. During that afternoon, as he sat at the bottom of the pit with Jacques, he had opened the book and read some of the poems to pass the time, many for the tenth or twentieth time. But there was one to which he kept returning. Something about it made him keep flipping the pages back. And only now, after Elwood Tucker had spoken and gone, after Bartlett had seen the guilt and the fear in his eyes, did Bartlett himself understand why.

'Listen, Jacques,' he said. In the flickering candlelight he opened the book and found the page. He leaned closer to the flame, in order to see the faded ink of the Ahsap's handwriting. Then he began to read.

I tripped one day and bumped my head,
When I awoke, my head was red.
Then someone asked what I had done—
He asked it in a tone of fun—
And I at once began to fear
That everyone would—

Jacques was laughing.

'No, listen,' said Bartlett. 'Don't laugh. Listen right to the end.'

And he began again.

I tripped one day and bumped my head,
When I awoke, my head was red.
Then someone asked what I had done—
He asked it in a tone of fun—
And I at once began to fear
That everyone would start to jeer

If they discovered that I'd slipped,
Tangled up my feet, and tripped,
And so I made them up a story:
I was brave, my exploits gory.

I said I'd fallen down a hole
Belonging to a handsome mole.
The mole conveyed me to a place
Where I at once came face to face
With three small heads whose name was Zig—
The heads were small, the jaws were big!
They kissed the mole, they hissed at me,
Then sang quite loud and scornfully:
'We'll eat you first, and after that,
We'll each take turns to wear your hat.
Then everyone will be our food,
Excluding children who are rude.'
This plan, I thought, contained a fate
That I preferred not to await.
I leapt on them, and with my fist,
I smashed a pair, the third I missed.
I caught him, though, and in the fight,
He bit me twice with all his might:
Once on the knee, once on the head,
And so, you see, my head is red.

That was the story that I told.
Each time I told, I grew more bold,
Inventing heads on left and right,
And legs and arms that joined the fight.

Then everyone cried out: 'Give Thanks!
He saved us from the jaws of cranks,
From being someone else's food,
Rewarding children who are rude.
Let's give him treasure, jewels in crates,
Knives and forks, his choice of plates.'
But I retreated from the crowd,
Their noise grew faint, my shame grew loud.
I wished I'd never bumped my head
Or said the things that I had said.
But now I saw it was too late,
For love can quickly turn to hate
When boasting's seen to be a lie—
So I must lie until I die.

Bartlett closed the book.

'Do you see, Jacques?' he said.

'Never follow a handsome mole?'

Bartlett shook his head.

'I'm not joking, Jacques. Can't you see what the Ahsap's saying? He needs to say sorry.'

'The Ahsap?'

'No. Be serious. Elwood!'

Jacques raised an eyebrow sceptically. Surely Bartlett didn't believe the Ahsap had written his poem about Elwood Tucker.

'He needs to admit what he did. He needs to admit he gave up, that he didn't perish in the forest like everyone thinks.'

Jacques still wasn't convinced. Elwood had already admitted it to *them*, and it hadn't seemed to make him much happier!

'Not to us, Jacques. To the world. To Sutton Pufrock, especially.'

Jacques frowned. 'Do you know what he told me?' said Jacques after a moment. 'When I met him, he said he hated Sutton Pufrock.'

Bartlett nodded. 'You see?'

Jacques picked up the Ahsap's book. He found the poem and began to read it again in the candlelight.

'He needs to say sorry,' said Bartlett. 'He needs the world to forgive him. That's the only way it's going to end.'

Jacques looked up.

'That's right, Jacques. The guilt. That's the only way he can bury it.' Bartlett looked around the stone well that was their prison. Their shadows wavered in the candlelight. 'But how do we make him realise it from down here?'

'Well, *that's* no problem. Gozo's on the job! He'll have us out of here in no time.'

They both smiled for a moment. Jacques held out the book and Bartlett took it. But already their smiles had gone. Jacques gazed up at the grille, trying to see, for the hundredth time that day, if there was any possibility of forcing a way through it—assuming he could get to it up the sheer walls of the pit, which he couldn't see any way of doing, either. And Bartlett opened the book, and frowned in the candlelight, glancing over the words that the Ahsap had written long before.

And all the time Elwood Tucker was pacing around the clearing, in two minds, unable to tear himself away, unable to go back inside the house to face the two explorers. Why couldn't he think clearly? He could find no peace. Locking them up had done nothing. In fact, it had made things worse. Just knowing they were there, at the bottom of that pit, was like a needle pressing into his flesh, and there was no relief from it.

Night had fallen. Moonlight made the Circle House pale and ghostly.

He stared at the house. A faint glow came from the doorway. They must have lit a candle, he thought. Around and around he paced, throwing glances at the house. How long could he leave them there? He didn't know how it was going to end. He had started something he couldn't control. But it must end, he knew that.

Somehow, it *must* end.

26

'You're going to carry me in *that*?' demanded the Falla, staring at the chair-and-poles contraption that Boas had built.

'*He's* the one we're going to carry?' demanded the WallBallers, staring at the great bulk of their Falla.

Everyone turned to look at Gozo and Muss. After a second, they were all shouting.

'*Impossible! . . . Never! . . . Him? . . . That?*'

'Quiet!' said Gozo, but no one could hear him—or no one cared if they did.

The shouting continued.

Suddenly there was a piercing, shrill note. It was so high, and so loud, and so piercing, that everyone stopped.

There was silence.

Anya took the flute away from her lips. She nodded at Gozo.

'The Falla has to go to the Circle House,' said Gozo. He turned to the WallBallers. 'We couldn't trust anyone to take him but you.' Then he turned to the Falla. 'This is the only way we could think of to get you there.'

The Falla looked at the chair. 'The only way they could think of . . .' he muttered to himself. 'Well, I'd like to know which of you came up with *this* brilliant idea.' But a moment later, still shaking his head with grave, very grave doubt, he began to raise himself from his couch. Everyone stood back, gazing at the dangerous and prolonged operation, hoping that if the Falla fell, he wouldn't fall on them.

Finally the Falla was up. He took a couple of steps to the chair. Everyone in the room could hear his knee bones grinding under his weight.

The Falla let himself down. 'It doesn't feel very safe,' he said.

'It's the biggest chair Uncle Boas had,' Muss explained.

The Falla didn't seem impressed.

'Come on,' said Gozo.

The WallBallers lined up around the poles. They divided into four pairs, two boys at each pole in front of the chair and two at each pole behind.

'All right,' said Gozo, looking over his shoulder from his position at the front of one of the poles. This was the big test, to see whether they were strong enough to lift the Falla, and whether the poles would break. 'Ready? Lift!'

They lifted, eight boys, all grimacing and straining.

'*Lift!*'

Slowly, the chair began to rise. It wobbled, tilted, and rose some more.

'That's enough! Enough!' cried the Falla, gripping the sides of the chair until his knuckles were white. '*Ohhhh!*' he wailed.

Gozo nodded at Anya, who was waiting in front of them, holding a torch. Anya led the way out of the room and into the winding passage that would take them to the exit from the building.

Branches loomed crazily, extending, clutching, twisting like the long dark fingers of enormous hands. Through their grasp, the light from Anya's torch floated like a bubble, and in that bubble came the Falla, borne by eight boys on his chair. And all around was darkness, the darkness of the trees, the grasping, lunging shadows of the branches.

Gozo just wished the Falla would stop wailing.

With every bump, every little bounce, he wailed into the night. Things had started badly. Getting through the passages in the Falla's house, with their twists and turns, their ups and downs, hadn't been easy. The Falla had taken a few knocks as the chair pitched and tilted against the walls like a ship on the waves. Between wails, he demanded to go back, and they might well have decided to turn around if anyone could have worked out how to do it in that narrow corridor. It was hard enough without having to listen to the Falla's complaints! Everyone was telling everyone else what to do. There was a lot of noise and shouting. By the time they got outside, the Falla was wailing so much that nothing could stop him.

But it was dangerous. As they moved through the trees, people would hear him. The expedition was meant to be a secret. The Falla was advertising it to everyone!

Faster, thought Gozo, we have to go faster. But the further they went along the path, the more they were slowing down. Gozo could feel it. They were getting tired. And the Circle House was still a long way off, perhaps they weren't even half way there yet.

'*Ohhhh!*' wailed the Falla, as the chair tilted again.

They righted it, but a minute later it began to tilt once more.

Now the chair began to scrape. It bumped.

'*Ohhhh! Ohhhh!*'

'Stop!' cried someone. 'Stop!'

They stopped just before the chair tipped right over.

It was Gandel who had halted them. Hardy, who was beside him, had let go. Now he collapsed and lay flat on his back beside the chair.

The Falla poked a toe towards Hardy. 'What's wrong with him?'

'Tired,' said Hardy, fighting for breath. 'Tired.'

'Well, he'd better get up,' said the Falla. 'We can't stop here.'

'Let's rest for a minute,' said Gandel. He sat down. The others sat down as well. The Falla watched them discontentedly, still sitting on his chair.

'We can't stop here,' said the Falla again.

'Gozo,' said Gandel, 'we're never going to make it to the Circle House. It's too far. The Falla's too heavy.'

Gandel was the strongest one there. If the Falla was too heavy for him, what chance did the rest of them have?

The Falla was silent. He might have been the Falla, but out here, he knew, he was helpless. If no one would carry him, he was stuck, like a beetle on its back.

Gozo glanced at the Falla. 'The Falla's right,' he said to Gandel, 'we can't stop here.'

Anya got up and took the torch to her father. She handed him her flute as well. Now her hands were free.

Gandel shook his head. 'We still won't be able to do it, Anya. We'll have to go for help.'

'We can't go for help!' exclaimed Gozo. 'It's a secret, Gandel. You know that.'

'Keeping it secret isn't going to get us there!'

Gandel looked around at the others. They nodded, one by one. Gozo glanced at Muss, who shrugged.

Maybe they were right, thought Gozo. But once they went to get others, he suspected, the whole thing would get out of control. All sorts of people would join in. They'd want to know *Why? When? Where?* Everything would start to get very complicated. The news would spread. So far, there was no sign of Elwood Tucker. But for how much longer?

'Let's rest a bit more,' said Gozo.

Gandel shrugged. That didn't solve the problem. Even after they'd rested, they still wouldn't be able to make it without help. Gozo was hoping for the impossible.

So they stayed there, the Falla on his chair, holding the torch, and everyone else sitting or lying on the ground. Time passed. This was no good as well. No one was happy. Some of them might even leave if nothing happened soon. Suddenly Gozo wished Bartlett were there. Bartlett would know what to do. Gozo tried to imagine what Bartlett would say. Inventiveness! Yes, but Gozo had Invented everything he could. Desperation and Perseverance! Yes, he had been Desperate, he had Persevered. He was still prepared to Persevere, but it

looked like everyone else was going to give up. Sutton
Pufrock probably had a saying for it. Something like:
'You have to know how much people can do. If you don't
know that . . .' Well, if you don't know that, you end
up on the ground in the middle of the forest with the
heaviest man in the world and seven other boys who are
too tired to carry him!

Gozo fell back on the path, like the others. He stared
up at the torchlight flickering across the branches of the
trees above him. The shadows of the branches rippled,
thinned and billowed, stretched and shortened, as if they
were performing a dance of their own. In the pit, he
thought, where Bartlett and Jacques were trapped, it
would be dark. He tried to imagine it. It wouldn't be
pleasant. Getting them out of there, that was what mattered. It didn't matter how he did it, as long as he did it.
All right, he thought, Gandel could go for help. If that
was the only way, what choice did he have?

Gozo sat up, but before he could say anything to Gandel, he heard a voice.

He turned around and saw a man standing in the pathway.

Pfister stared at the chair in amazement. 'Falla!' he repeated.

'Pfister, get off the track!' said the Falla. 'Can't you see you're standing in our way.'

Pfister glanced around at the boys sprawled on the ground.

'Your way where, Falla?'

'To the Circle House.'

Pfister's eyes narrowed. 'You don't want to go there, Falla.'

'Yes, I do.'

'No, you don't. There's nothing to see there.'

'What about Bartlett and Jacques le Grand?'

'Who are they?'

'*Pfister . . .*' growled the Falla.

'Oh, them? Bartlett and Jacques? No, I don't know where they are. Elwood knows. Ask him. They've gone. Gone.'

'Gone where?'

'I don't know, Falla.'

'Pfister, are you lying to me?'

Pfister hesitated. 'I don't know, Falla.'

The Falla looked at the boys on the ground. 'Get up!' he roared suddenly. 'Pfister, help them!'

'Help them what, Falla?'

'Help them carry me.'

'But I promised Elwood—'

'You *promised* Elwood? So you're keeping promises now, are you, Pfister?'

'Trying to, Falla,' Pfister mumbled sheepishly.

'Pfister, I don't care what you promised Elwood. And I don't care what Elwood told you to do.'

Pfister stared at the Falla with his mouth open. 'You don't care what Elwood told me to do?'

The boys were wearily taking their places at the poles. The Falla handed the torch back to Anya.

'At the back, Pfister. No arguments!!'

Pfister went behind the chair. He stood between the poles and took one in each hand. 'This looks awfully heavy,' he whispered to Bertram, who was standing in front of him. Bertram nodded silently.

Gozo looked over his shoulder at the Falla. The Falla nodded.

'Ready? *Lift!*'

The Circle House was ahead of them at the end of the path. They could see it in the moonlight, pale, its doorway a dark gap punched out of the wall. Now they surged towards it with the chair, forgetting the weight of the Falla, the ache in their arms and the tiredness in their legs, imagining, as they came out of the trees, that nothing stood between them and their goal.

But Elwood Tucker had already seen them coming.

All this time, he had been in the clearing, standing, pacing, pacing, standing, for hours, unable to bring himself to leave, unable to go back inside. He wasn't waiting for the Falla to arrive. He didn't know the Falla was coming. He wasn't waiting for anything. He just didn't know what to do. He was lost. This wasn't the Elwood Tucker that anyone else would have recognised. It wasn't the Elwood Tucker that *Elwood Tucker* would have recognised. But when a man reaches this point he is dangerous. He's unpredictable, capable of doing things that no one would have any reason to expect from him.

He saw the light of the Falla's arrival when it was still far off in the trees. At once, like a wolf disturbed on the prowl, he was alert. He looked around, then retreated from the clearing. From the shadows of the trees, he watched the Falla being carried to the house. His lips curled in a faint, almost grim smile at the sight. It was an inventive way to bring the Falla, he granted that. Who had thought of it? Bartlett? Jacques? There was bitter relief in his smile as well. The Falla would have found out eventually. Good, let it be now! Let them finish it. Soon. The sooner the better.

He watched the procession as it reached the house. The Falla was carried inside. Now Elwood Tucker crept forward. He reached the house and hugged the wall. He heard the voices, shouts of amazement, as everyone looked into the pit. 'You were right,' he heard the Falla say to Gozo. 'You were right. I should have believed you.'

He heard the Falla tell Pfister to go to the doorway, where there was a lever concealed in the stone. But he knew what would happen, and he waited for it, grinning. Pfister found the lever, but it didn't work. The Falla shouted at him, telling him to pull it harder. Elwood Tucker could hardly keep from laughing out loud, imagining the scene inside.

'You've broken it!'

'No I haven't, Falla. Look. It wasn't connected to anything.'

There was silence, and then the Falla's voice, low, puzzled. 'Someone's tampered with it.'

Yes, thought Elwood Tucker, someone's tampered with it. And who could that be, Falla?

'It's five years since I was here,' said the Falla. 'There was only one other person who knew about that mechanism.'

'That's right, only one other person,' said Elwood Tucker, and he walked through the doorway, and everyone in the room turned to see his bald head gleaming in the torchlight, his figure silhouetted against the darkness of the night outside.

27

At the bottom of the pit, Bartlett and Jacques tried to follow what was happening. The silence was loud, tense, meaningful, as meaningful as any words that might have been used in its place.

Finally the Falla spoke.

'Let them out, Elwood.'

Then there was silence again. Now Elwood Tucker appeared above the grille. He looked down at the two explorers coldly.

'Let them out, Elwood,' said the Falla again.

Elwood Tucker turned back to him. His muscles were tensed, his fingers twitched. Every eye in the room was on him. Suddenly Gozo wondered whether he would spring, whether he had a knife and was going to pull it out and leap at the Falla.

But the Falla's voice was steady. 'What are you going to do, Elwood? Are you going to attack me? And Pfister? And everybody else?'

Gozo didn't think this was the time to be putting ideas into Elwood Tucker's head!

Tucker glanced fleetingly around the room, as if weighing his chances against everyone who was there.

'Let them out now. What are you going to do? How is it going to end?'

Now Tucker replied. 'Ask them! They'll leave, I'm warning you.'

'Let them out.'

'They'll leave,' hissed Tucker.

The Falla shrugged.

The two men gazed at one another, the fat man in his chair, the lean, bald man who faced him across the grille. The seconds that passed were long, slow. It was as if a coin were spinning, and presently it must fall on one side or the other, give one of two results. Suddenly something happened to Elwood Tucker's face. A flicker of the muscles, like a ripple slipping across the surface of a lake, and then it was gone. The ex-explorer threw back his head and closed his eyes for an instant. In that instant it was as if the coin fell. When he opened his eyes, the danger in his gaze had disappeared.

He took a few steps towards the door. He pressed on something with his toe, and at the same time, with his hand, triggered something in the wall. A moment later, there was a loud grinding sound.

The grille slid back, Bartlett and Jacques rocketed into view, and the two explorers were sitting on the stone in the middle of the room once more, as if they had never budged.

But they budged now! They jumped off that stone as if it were white-hot.

The Falla looked at them gravely. 'As the Falla of Run,' he said, 'I owe you a deep apology. To both of you, Bartlett and Jacques.'

'I don't suppose there are any other tricks in this house we should know about?' said Bartlett.

'I don't think so,' said the Falla. He looked at Elwood

Tucker. Elwood shook his head.

'Well, that's all right,' said Bartlett. 'Apology accepted.'

Jacques nodded. Apology accepted.

'But there is one thing I need to know,' continued the Falla. 'I mean . . . I would like to know. What are you going to do? Are you planning to leave?'

'Yes,' said Bartlett.

Pfister and the WallBallers stared in astonishment at these men who said they were going to leave Run. Anya glanced hurriedly at Gozo.

'You see, Falla,' said Elwood Tucker harshly. 'I told you that's what they'd do.'

'We never stop people leaving,' said the Falla to Bartlett. 'I mean, we've never had to.'

'Are you going to start now?' said Bartlett.

'I don't think so,' said the Falla. 'I don't think . . . that's not the kind of thing we want to start doing in Run.'

'No. I agree. It isn't,' said Bartlett.

'But we do have a problem,' said the Falla. 'Elwood has a point . . .'

'Thank you, Falla!' said Elwood sarcastically.

'You see, Bartlett, the reason we live here so peacefully is that no one suspects we're here. Can you imagine what would happen if people heard there was a lost city in the forest? Suddenly we'd have hundreds of greedy adventurers coming to find gold. Don't shake your head—it's true. If I think back to the way I was when I was younger, I would have come myself if I'd heard about such a place. And there *is* no gold, as you can see. None that we've ever found, anyway. I'm glad there isn't. What would we do with it? It's things that are scarce that make people greedy. When there's enough for everybody, everybody has enough.'

'We could tell people there's no gold,' offered Bartlett.

The Falla shook his head. 'That wouldn't work. People would think you were just trying to protect it for yourself. I know how the world is, Bartlett. I wasn't born here, I was born outside. No, rumours would spread. We'd be overrun. So I'm going to ask you a favour, Mr Bartlett. And you too, Jacques. If you're going to leave, we won't stop you. But when you go back, please don't say anything about Run. If people ask you what you found, just say . . . say you found nothing.'

Gozo wondered what Bartlett was going to say. He saw him glance at Jacques. Jacques shrugged, then shook his head.

'I'm afraid it's not so simple,' said Bartlett, turning back to the Falla. 'You see, there's a rule explorers follow: they have to tell the truth about what they find. There's no one else to check on them, you see, when they come back from a place no one else has ever explored.'

'I see,' said the Falla, and the WallBallers nodded, because it was obvious, once you thought about it.

'If you can't trust an explorer to tell the truth,' added Bartlett, 'you can't trust the sun to rise or the rain to fall. A very great explorer used to say that. His name was Sutton Pufrock, and he taught me everything I know.'

'Not Sutton Pufrock! We don't want to hear about Sutton *Pufrock*!' cried Elwood Tucker.

'He taught Elwood everything he knew, as well,' said Bartlett quietly. 'Only Elwood seems to have forgotten quite a lot of it.'

The Falla frowned. 'What are we going to do, Bartlett?'

'I don't know.'

No one seemed to know. Gozo frowned, trying to think of an answer. Inventiveness, he was beginning to understand, came in all shapes and forms, and here was another one.

Finally it was Jacques le Grand who broke the silence. He spoke in a low voice, almost reluctantly, as if what he had to say were meant only for Bartlett . . . but he didn't mind if other people heard it as well.

'Bartlett, do you think Sutton Pufrock ever discovered a place that would have been destroyed if he had followed the rule? A place that would have been destroyed because he told what he knew about it? A place,' added Jacques carefully, 'that would have been destroyed if he told *everything* he knew about it?'

Bartlett thought. 'I don't know,' he said to Jacques.

Jacques didn't say anything else. He didn't need to. Perhaps Sutton Pufrock would have allowed an exception to the rule, had he ever found a reason to make one. But you don't find yourself in a place like Run every day, or every year, or even once in every lifetime, even if you spend that whole lifetime exploring, and maybe Sutton Pufrock never did. Or maybe he *had* found himself in such a place, once, and that was precisely the reason no one knew about it!

Bartlett looked back at the Falla. 'We won't tell about Run,' he said. 'Right, Jacques?'

Jacques nodded.

'What will you say?' asked the Falla.

'We'll say we didn't find anything to go looking for in the forest. That's the truth, isn't it? If it's gold people are after, they won't find any here.'

'But what if they ask you something specific? What if they ask you, for instance, if you met anyone?'

'I don't know, Falla. We'll think about that when we get to it.'

'Oh, this is ridiculous!' cried Elwood Tucker. He came forward. 'Why do you believe what they're saying? The minute they get out of here they'll be talking.'

'I believe them,' said the Falla. 'You know them better than me, Elwood. Don't you trust them?'

Elwood Tucker scoffed. The problem was, he did trust them. They were just the kind of characters who would always do exactly what they promised—that had always been one of the most irritating things about them!

'Besides,' said the Falla, in a mischievous tone, 'if they were going to say anything they wanted, they would have promised to be quiet in the first place, just to get away.'

Bartlett grinned. The Falla was absolutely right!

'Well,' said the Falla, 'that's settled. You're welcome to stay here in Run as long as you like. And when you're ready to leave, then—'

'Actually, Falla,' said Bartlett, 'it's not *all* settled.'

Elwood Tucker was the taller, Bartlett the stringlier, and now the two men faced each other, at last, after all these years.

'What do you want us to say, Elwood?' asked Bartlett.

'I thought we'd already worked that out!' exclaimed the Falla in dismay.

Bartlett didn't reply. Elwood knew what he was he talking about. It had nothing to do with the Falla, or Run, and for the moment, as far as Bartlett and Elwood Tucker were concerned, they might as well have been entirely alone in that room, with only Jacques le Grand standing behind Bartlett's shoulder.

'What difference does it make, what I want you to say?' demanded Elwood bitterly. 'If you can't trust an explorer to tell the truth, you can't trust the sun or the rain, right, Bartlett?'

'That's right, Elwood. You're an explorer. You know it as well as I do.'

'*Was.* I *was* an explorer, Bartlett.'

'You still are, Elwood. You always will be.'

Elwood Tucker gazed into Bartlett's eyes, searching, trying to see whether he really meant it.

'Elwood, we're not judging you. I told you that before. It was your decision. We all have to make our own decisions. No one's judging you for it.'

Elwood was silent for a moment longer. 'What do you have in mind that you might say?' he murmured eventually.

'Well, we could say that you . . . retired.'

'Where?'

Bartlett shrugged.

'You can't just say I retired in Run. No one will know what you mean. You'll end up telling them everything.'

Bartlett thought about that. He glanced at Jacques. 'We could say we heard you retired, Elwood, but we didn't know exactly where. We could say we heard you retired a long time ago, and you hadn't perished, and you're living very happily, and are content.'

Elwood frowned.

'Bartlett,' said the Falla, 'there's a man called Elwood Tucker I'd like to tell you about. He retired a long time ago, and he didn't perish, and he's living very happily, and he's content.'

Bartlett nodded. Now he'd heard it. But he still waited, looking at Elwood.

Jacques saw Bartlett reach into his pocket, where he had put the Ahsap's book. Suddenly Jacques had a horrible thought! But fortunately Elwood spoke before Bartlett had the chance to read everyone the poem about the heads called Zig.

'Tell them I'm sorry,' whispered Elwood.

'Yes,' said Bartlett.

'Tell them I'm sorry I didn't tell them, but it was hard, from where I . . . retired. It was hard to get word to them, and I'm sorry if anyone thought I perished, and . . . tell Sutton Pufrock. Tell him I'm sorry, Bartlett. And tell him I crossed the forest. Tell him that. Tell him it's called the Forest of Plenty . . . and I explored it, all the way to the sea. I've always wanted him to know.'

'He'll appreciate that,' whispered Bartlett hoarsely, 'he's always wanted to know.'

Elwood nodded. The light, gleaming in his eye, almost made it look as if there were tears there, but Bartlett couldn't be sure, because there were almost tears in his eyes as well!

Suddenly Bartlett took a step forward and he grabbed Elwood and he hugged him, he didn't know why, and Elwood hugged him back. The feeling was just as it had been when they were young, very young, when Sutton Pufrock was their teacher and they were jealous of each other and liked each other at the same time, when they would race each other to be first but stop to pick the other up if he had fallen.

'You were good, Elwood,' said Bartlett, standing back again and looking him in the eye.

'You were tough, Bartlett.'

'I was good as well.'

Elwood Tucker nodded. 'You still are.' He threw a glance at Jacques. 'Even Jacques is.'

Jacques rolled his eyes. Elwood Tucker, always the

expert, even when he hadn't been on an exploration in ten years!

'Maybe you just took our rivalry a bit too far,' said Bartlett.

'Me? What about *you?*' demanded Elwood Tucker. 'Do you remember the Mosely Cave? Do you remember what you did that day, Bartlett?'

'That was twenty-five years ago! We were boys. If we're going to talk about the Mosely Cave, let's not forget the Agron Falls. Do you remember what *you* did there?'

'The Agron Falls? What about the Lenster Cusp?'

'Barton's Sound!'

'Frobisher's Gully!'

'Peswick's Peak!'

'Excuse me,' said the Falla anxiously, 'this was all going so well. Perhaps we shouldn't think so much about the past. The past is gone. The past is finished. The past is . . .' The Falla didn't go on. He didn't need to. Bartlett and Tucker were laughing.

Suddenly Tucker frowned. 'I can't remember a Peswick's Peak.'

'Neither can I,' said Bartlett, 'I made it up!'

Even Jacques laughed at that. Everyone else watched, puzzled, as the three explorers grinned and roared. Finally their laughter subsided.

Bartlett was looking at Elwood Tucker again. 'It's all right, Elwood,' he said quietly. 'It is, really.'

Elwood gazed at him for a moment, and then he nodded.

'Well, I'm not going to pretend I understand exactly

what's going on between you two,' said the Falla, 'but as long as you're both happy, so am I. And there's someone else you should be happy with. Him!' he said, and he pointed directly at Gozo.

Bartlett grinned.

'Yes. I may be an old Falla, but that boy taught me a few things tonight. He taught me about listening to the truth, and finding ways to get things done.'

'We call it Inventiveness,' said Bartlett. 'And Desperation and Perseverance.'

'Well, if that's what you call it, that's what he's got. And if that's what he needs,' added the Falla, 'he's going to go far.'

Gozo didn't know what to do! He blushed, and grinned, and when he glanced at Anya, he just blushed even more.

In the meantime, the Falla had turned to the Wall-Ballers. 'Well, what are you waiting for? Carry me back!'

The WallBallers groaned. All the way back to the Falla's house! Their arms were aching and their legs were heavy.

Bartlett glanced at Jacques. Jacques shrugged. After all, they'd been locked up for the whole day. They could use some exercise!

'Elwood?' said Bartlett. 'Come on. Let's show them what explorers can do!'

The three men took the poles of the chair and lifted it briskly into the air. The Falla felt perfectly safe in their hands and didn't even wail. But if this was a job for explorers, Gozo wasn't going to be left out. Besides, he was going to finish what he had started! He grabbed hold of the pole in front of Bartlett. And then Muss decided he didn't want to be left out either, and Gandel joined him, and in a minute all the WallBallers were jostling to get a hand on the poles. Pfister slapped his forehead and exclaimed that he had promised to help carry the Falla back. The chair was pitching and rocking again, and in the time it took Bartlett to sort everybody out so they all had a place, the Falla did let out one tiny little wail, although it was really more of a squeak.

Then they carried the chair out of the house, only to discover that someone must have observed the Falla wailing on his way to the Circle House, and in the time they had been inside, word had spread and half of Run had arrived to see what was happening. All over the clearing, torches flickered in the light, and when they saw that it was the Falla on the chair, people pressed up close to talk to him, people who hadn't seen him for years and years, ever since he had grown too fat to walk. They followed him all the way back to his house, and when they arrived, the Falla sat outside for a while, and talked to them some more.

'Perhaps,' murmured the Falla in Elwood Tucker's ear, 'if we can put a few cushions on this chair, and find some people who can carry it without tipping me over, I might start to use it.'

'How often?' said Elwood.

'I don't know,' said the Falla. 'Perhaps every day.'

28

As it turned out, Muss and Gozo were right when they told Boas that the pole-chair was going to be used in the Crow Performance, although, when they said it, they had no idea what part it was going to play. The Falla was carried in it at the head of the procession, all the way from the HoneyCone, where it started, to the ruined Round Tower, where the Performance took place, and where everybody feasted long into the night. Since no one had seen the Falla come out of his house for years, it caused a sensation, and by the end of the day Boas had already agreed to build a larger, more comfortable chair, and there was talk of a foot-rest and cushions. Grandma Myrtle, who told her brother it was about *time* he came out again, couldn't quite disguise her happiness at seeing him once more, and offered to embroider the cushions with Lou-Lou birds.

The Crow Performance was interesting, but the main point of the day, it seemed, was the feast. Even the performers were anxious to get to the food. Nothing was ordinary. Each dish was a delicacy, more tantalising than the one before. In addition to the traditional specialties of Run, seven new recipes had been invented for the occasion, as custom demanded, and everyone agreed that at least five of them would become regular favourites. And there was the special sweet called klepko, which was made with the honey of a certain rare species of bee.

So rare was this bee, and so little honey did it produce, that klepko was made only once a year, for the Crow Feast, and each person's share was rationed by Meria, the sweetmaker, who fiercely guarded the table on which it was kept. But that was the only thing that *was* rationed. If there were any doubt that this was the Forest of Plenty, you had only to look at the groaning tables of the Crow Feast, from which you could take as much as you wanted, again and again and again, until it was physically impossible to eat any more.

And this is what people did, because that's what a feast is for. Bartlett and Jacques and Gozo, in order to avoid appearing ungrateful for the hospitality of Run, had no choice but to join in as heartily as the others!

The following day was devoted to the WallBall tournament. Everyone went to watch, even those who still felt sick from all the food they had eaten the day before. Once again, the Falla was carried there in his new chair. The grassy slopes along the court were crowded with spectators. Gozo was going to play, Muss insisted. The games went on all day. Their team didn't win, it was one of the older groups that triumphed. But everyone said they had played well, and their team would certainly win the Crow tournament one year. And Gandel, they said, had exceptional talent, and might even be named as a member of the Team of Teams, which was selected each year to reward the best players. And Gozo, they said, really was dangerous on the forward angle, far more dangerous than you could expect from someone who had arrived from the desert only a month before.

But there was only one person Gozo was playing for. What she thought mattered more to him than everyone else's opinions put together.

That night, when the tournament ended, Bartlett, Jacques and Gozo said goodbye to the Falla, and to Grandma Myrtle, and to the woodcutter twins, and to the other people they had met in Run. They said goodbye to Elwood Tucker. And early the next morning, almost as soon as the sun had risen, they were on the move.

The explorers were ready for the forest once again. Their bags bulged with corn biscuits and smoked turkey, their machetes had been sharpened. Muss came with them as far as the WallBall court. He gave Gozo a WallBall to keep, and just before they parted, he whispered something in Gozo's ear. It was the new rule Muss had devised. Gozo nodded appreciatively. In his opinion, it was an excellent rule, and he suggested that Muss should tell the Falla as soon as he could.

Then they said goodbye, and Gozo kept glancing over his shoulder until the trees blocked Muss from view, and Muss kept waving at him until he disappeared.

Pfister came with them a little way longer, and then he said goodbye as well, saying he had promised to collect nuts for Meria the sweetmaker, who hadn't a single one left after all the sweets she had made for the Crow Feast. But he could collect them tomorrow, he added, if they needed him to come with them any further. Bartlett grinned, and told him they could manage. So Pfister left

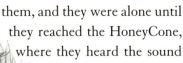

them, and they were alone until they reached the HoneyCone, where they heard the sound of a flute, and they stopped.

Gozo went up the stairs. Bartlett and Jacques waited in the clearing. The sound of the flute died away. The minutes passed. The noise of the birds from the trees was very loud, as it always was this early in the morning. Eventually they saw Gozo coming down the stairs again. His head was bowed, his eyes downcast, and his steps were short and unwilling.

He was holding something in his hand.

'Anya gave this to me. Grandma Myrtle wants you to have it,' he said tonelessly to Bartlett, and he held it out.

Bartlett took it. It was a tapestry of a Lou-Lou bird. It showed the bird sitting on a branch, with its beak poised over a luscious fruit.

'I thanked her for you,' said Gozo.

Bartlett packed the tapestry into his pack.

'Are you ready, Gozo?'

Gozo nodded. His lip was trembling.

Bartlett glanced at Jacques. They didn't say anything. They began to walk towards the forest.

'I'll never meet another girl like her,' cried Gozo suddenly, as they reached the first of the trees. 'Never!'

'Maybe not,' said Bartlett.

'Mr Bartlett!' cried Gozo. That wasn't what he expected to hear. He expected to be told he'd meet lots of other girls like Anya, or even nicer ones. That was the kind of thing other people always said. He'd often heard his uncle Mordi say something just like it to one of his sons, whenever there was a girl who decided she didn't want to see one of them any more.

'Just be thankful you did meet her,' said Bartlett.

'Do you think I'll ever see her again?' demanded Gozo hopefully. 'Is there any chance?'

Bartlett shrugged. 'Who knows? Nothing's impossible.'

Jacques was pulling out his machete. Bartlett took his blade out as well. The forest was closing in on them again.

'We'll have to get you one of these when we get a chance,' said Bartlett.

'A machete?' said Gozo.

'Why not? You're an explorer now.'

'Am I?' demanded Gozo excitedly.

'Of course you are,' said Bartlett. 'Inventiveness, Desperation, Perseverance. You used them all. In fact, I suspect Jacques owes you an apology. He didn't believe you'd do it.'

'That's all right, Jacques,' said Gozo. 'Neither did I!'

Bartlett grinned. 'Jacques?' he called out.

'Sorry,' said Jacques, who was already ahead of them, hacking out a path. He sliced the end off a branch with a mighty heave of his blade.

'Actually,' said Gozo, biting his lip. 'I really wasn't so

Inventive. You know, the poles to carry the chair . . . that was . . . well, I had some help. It was Anya's idea.'

'Does this mean I can take back my apology?' called out Jacques.

Bartlett laughed. 'Gozo, what the Falla said was absolutely right. You taught him a lesson. It doesn't matter how much help you had. We all have help. It's knowing what help to take, and when, that's the trick. And you certainly knew.'

Gozo thought about that. Bartlett was right, he decided.

'You still have a lot to learn, of course,' said Bartlett.

'Of course, Mr Bartlett! Of course I do.' Gozo paused for a moment. 'Does that mean you're going to teach me?'

Bartlett grinned. 'Come on, Jacques, why so slow?' he called out, and he stepped forward to help Jacques hack and slash at the trees, driving a path through the shadowy world of the forest floor, searching for a brook that would take them to a stream, which would take them to a creek, which would take them to the river that would lead them back to the Gircassian Rift. They weren't going to cross the forest to the coast, Elwood Tucker had explored it years before.

'Mr Bartlett,' said Gozo', 'I was wondering . . . Are you really going to say nothing about Run, like you told the Falla?'

'You heard what I said, Gozo. I promised the Falla. And if you can't trust an explorer to tell the truth, you can't . . .'

'I know. I know that, Mr Bartlett. But if you don't tell about Run, you're not telling the truth to other people, are you? And that's just as bad as breaking your promise to the Falla, isn't it?'

Bartlett stopped. Jacques had turned back as well. Now they both looked at Gozo.

'Some things aren't simple, Gozo,' said Bartlett.

Behind Bartlett's shoulder, Jacques nodded.

'Sometimes, there are two things that seem right, but you can't do them both. How do you choose?'

Gozo waited, expecting another one of Sutton Pufrock's sayings. But for once, there wasn't one that suited.

'I don't know,' said Bartlett. 'But I will tell you one thing, Gozo. I've seen a lot of the world, more than your average explorer, but I've never seen a place like Run. Neither has Jacques. I've never seen a place that's so peaceful . . . so happy. Hidden away from everything, undisturbed. If you ask me, the world needs at least one place like that. To do anything to destroy it would be a terrible thing. Much worse than bending the rules, just this one time. Just once.'

'Even iron bends,' added Jacques, as a certain old man, called Prule, had said to him once before.

Bartlett grinned. 'Exactly. Now, why are we thinking about the past? Let's think about the future. We're explorers! Where are we going? What do you suggest, Jacques? The Forest of Krill?'

'Not *another* forest!' cried Gozo. 'We're not even out of this one yet!'

Bartlett sighed, as if he were very reluctant to give up the chance of going straight to another forest. 'Well, we could go the Bascarry Islands,' he said, 'where they say volcanoes turn the night sky red . . .'

'And giant turtles lay eggs the colour of plums,' added Jacques.

Gozo's eyes were wide with wonder.

'Yes, I suppose we could go there,' said Bartlett, as Jacques turned and led them forward again. 'I wonder what Grandma Myrtle would make of turtles like that, Gozo? More perfect than the Lou-Lou?'

'I doubt she'd agree, Mr Bartlett.'

'You're probably right. It was nice of her to give us that tapestry. I'm sure it meant a lot to her.'

'She said it was almost perfect,' said Gozo.

'And Anya, didn't she give you anything to remember her by?'

Gozo didn't reply.

'Gozo?'

Gozo was going red. Bartlett and Jacques had stopped again, and they were both looking at him.

'No secrets!' said Bartlett. 'No secrets between explorers, right, Jacques? Now, what did she give you?'

'Something,' murmured Gozo.

Bartlett and Jacques glanced knowingly at each other. Gozo could see the grins starting on their faces.

'Something you'll remember?' said Bartlett.

Gozo nodded. It was something he'd remember as long as he lived.